The Busybody

A Comedy

SUSANNA CENTLIVRE

RENARD PRESS

RENARD PRESS LTD

Kemp House
152–160 City Road
London EC1V 2NX
United Kingdom
info@renardpress.com
020 8050 2928

www.renardpress.com

The Busybody first published in 1709
'Prefatory Remarks' first published in 1819
This edition first published by Renard Press Ltd in 2022

Cover design by Will Dady

ISBN: 978-1-913724-67-2

CONTENTS

PREFATORY REMARKS

The Busy Body is a comedy that has now held possession of the stage above a hundred years (the best test of excellence), and the merit that has enabled it to do so consists in the ingenuity of the contrivance, the liveliness of the plot and the striking effect of the situations. Mrs Centlivre, in this and her other plays, could do nothing without a stratagem; but she could do everything with one. She delights in putting her dramatis personae continually at their wit's end, and in helping them off with a new evasion; and the subtlety of her resources is in proportion to the criticalness of the situation and the shortness of the notice for resorting to an expedient. Twenty times in seeing or reading one of her plays your pulse beats quick, and you become restless and apprehensive for the event; but with a fine theatrical sleight of hand, she lets you off, undoes the knot of the difficulty, and you breathe freely again, and have a hearty laugh into the bargain. In short, with her knowledge of chambermaids' tricks, and insight into the intricate foldings of lovers' hearts, she plays with the events of comedy, as a juggler shuffles about a pack of cards, to serve his own purposes, and to the surprise of the spectator. This is one of the most delightful employments of the dramatic art.

It costs nothing but a voluntary tax on the inventive powers of the author; and it produces, when successfully done, profit and praise to one party and pleasure to all. To show the extent and importance of theatrical amusements (which some grave persons would decry altogether, and which no one can extol too highly), a friend of ours, whose name will be as well known to posterity as it is to his contemporaries, was not long ago mentioning that one of the earliest and most memorable impressions ever made on his mind was the seeing *Venice Preserved** acted in a country town when he was only nine years old. But he added that an elderly lady who took him to see it lamented, notwithstanding the wonder and delight he experienced, that instead of *Venice Preserved* they had not gone to see *The Busybody*, which had been acted the night before. This was fifty years ago, since which, and for fifty years before that, it has been acted a thousand times in town and country, giving delight to the old, the young and middle-aged, passing the time carelessly, and affording matter for agreeable reflection afterwards, making us think ourselves, and wish to be thought, the men equal to Sir George Airy in grace and spirit, the women to Miranda and Isabinda in love and beauty, and all of us superior to Marplot in wit. Among the scenes that might be mentioned in this comedy as striking instances of happy stage effect are Miranda's contrivance to escape from Sir George by making him turn his back upon her to hear her confession of love, and the ludicrous attitude in which he is left waiting for the rest of her speech after the lady has vanished; his offer of the hundred pounds to her guardian to make love to her in his presence, and, when she receives him in dumb show, his answering for both; his situation concealed behind the chimney screen, his supposed metamorphosis into a monkey and his deliverance from thence, in that character, by the interference of Marplot; Mrs Patch's sudden conversion of the mysterious love letter into a charm for the toothache, and the whole of Marplot's meddling and blunders. The last character is taken from Dryden and the Duchess of Newcastle;* and is indeed the only attempt at character in the play. It is amusing and superficial. We see little of the puzzled perplexity of his brain, but his actions are absurd enough. He whiffles about the stage with considerable volubility, and makes a very lively automaton. Sir George Airy sets out for a scene or two in a spirited manner, but afterwards the character evaporates in the name; and he becomes as commonplace as his friend Charles, who merely laments over his misfortunes or gets out of them by following the suggestions of his valet or his valet's mistress. Miranda is the heroine of the piece, and has a right to be so, for she is a beauty and an heiress. Her friend has less to recommend her; but who can refuse to fall in love with her name? What volumes of sighs, what a world of love, is breathed in the very sound alone – the letters that form the charming name of Isabinda!

WILLIAM HAZLITT
1819

TO THE RIGHT HONOURABLE

JOHN LORD SOMERS,

*Lord-President of Her Majesty's Most Honourable Privy Council.**

May it please your lordship,
As it's an established custom in these latter ages for all writers, particularly the poetical, to shelter their productions under the protection of the most distinguished, whose approbation produces a kind of inspiration, much superior to that which the heathenish poets* pretended to derive from their fictitious Apollo:* so it was my ambition to address one of my weak performances to your lordship, who, by universal consent,[1] are justly allowed to be the best judge of all kinds of writing.

I was indeed at first deterred from my design by a thought that it might be accounted unpardonable rudeness to obtrude a trifle of this nature to a person whose sublime wisdom moderates that council* which, at this critical juncture, overrules the fate of all Europe. But then I was encouraged

1 *consent*: Agreement.

by reflecting that Lelius and Scipio,* the two greatest men in their time among the Romans, both for political and military virtues in the height of their important affairs, thought the perusal and improving of Terence's* comedies the noblest way of unbinding their minds. I own I were guilty of the highest vanity should I presume to put my composures in parallel with those of that celebrated dramatist. But then again, I hope that your lordship's native goodness and generosity in condescension to the taste of the best and fairest part of the town, who have been pleased to be diverted by the following scenes, will excuse and overlook such faults as your nicer judgement might discern.

And here, my lord, the occasion seems fair for me to engage in a panegyric[1] upon those natural and acquired abilities which so brightly adorn your person: but I shall resist that temptation, being conscious of the inequality of a female pen to so masculine an attempt; and having no other ambition than to subscribe myself,

My lord,

Your lordship's

Most humble and

Most obedient servant,

SUSANNA CENTLIVRE

1 *panegyric*: A public speech in praise of someone.

PROLOGUE

By the author of
TUNBRIDGE WALKS*

Though modern prophets were exposed of late,*
The author could not prophesy his fate;
If with such scenes an audience had been fired,
The poet must have really been inspired.
But these, alas! are melancholy days
For modern prophets, and for modern plays.
Yet since prophetic lies please fools o' fashion,
And women are so fond of agitation,
To men of sense, I'll prophesy anew,
And tell you wondrous things that will prove true:
  Undaunted colonels will to camps repair,
Assured there'll be no skirmishes this year.
  On our own terms will flow the wished-for peace;
All wars, except 'twixt man and wife, will cease.*
The grand monarch may wish his son a throne,
But hardly will advance to lose his own.*
This season most things bear a smiling face;
But players in summer have a dismal case,*
Since your appearance only is our act of grace.*
Court ladies will to country seats be gone –
My lord can't all the year live great in town –

Where, wanting operas, basset[1] and a play,
They'll sigh and stitch a gown to pass the time away.
Gay city wives* at Tunbridge* will appear,
Whose husbands long have laboured for an heir;
Where many a courtier may their wants relieve,
But by the waters only they conceive.*
The Fleet Street sempstress,[2] toast of Temple sparks,
That runs spruce[3] neckcloths for attorneys' clerks,
At Cupid's Gardens* will her hours regale,
Sing 'Fair Dorinda'* and drink bottled ale.
At all assemblies, rakes[4] are up and down,
And gamesters, where they think they are not known.
  Should I denounce our author's fate today,
To cry down prophecies, you'd damn the play.
Yet whims like these have sometimes made you laugh;
'Tis tattling all, like Isaac Bickerstaff.*
  Since war and places claim the bards that write,*
Be kind, and bear a woman's treat tonight;
Let your indulgence all her fears allay,
And none but woman-haters damn this play.

---

1 *basset*: A high-risk card game played only by the nobility and very wealthy.
2 *sempstress*: Seamstress.
3 *runs spruce*: Spruces up, fixes quickly.
4 *rakes*: Libertines.

THE BUSYBODY

A COMEDY

As it is acted at the

THEATRE ROYAL

IN DRURY LANE

by Her Majesty's servants

WRITTEN BY

MRS SUSANNA CENTLIVRE

Quem tulit ad scenam ventoso gloria curru,
Exanimat lentus spectator, sedulus inflat.
Sic leve, sic parvum est, animum quod laudis avarum
Subruit aut reficit—

HORAT. EPIST. LIB. II. EP. I*

CHARACTERS

SIR GEORGE AIRY, *a gentleman of four thousand a year, in love with* MIRANDA

SIR FRANCIS GRIPE, *guardian to* MIRANDA *and* MARPLOT, *father to* CHARLES, *in love with* MIRANDA

CHARLES, *friend to* SIR GEORGE, *in love with* ISABINDA

SIR JEALOUS TRAFFICK, *a merchant that had lived some time in Spain, a great admirer of the Spanish customs, father to* ISABINDA

MARPLOT, *a sort of a silly fellow, cowardly, but very inquisitive to know everybody's business, generally spoils all he undertakes, yet without design*

WHISPER, *servant to* CHARLES

MIRANDA, *an heiress, worth thirty thousand pounds, really in love with* SIR GEORGE, *but pretends to be so with her guardian* SIR FRANCIS

ISABINDA, *daughter to* SIR JEALOUS, *in love with* CHARLES, *but designed for a Spanish merchant by her father, and kept up from the sight of all men*

PATCH, *her woman*

SCENTWELL, *woman to* MIRANDA

SERVANTS

BUTLER

DRAWER*

ACT I

SCENE I

*The park.** SIR GEORGE AIRY *meeting* CHARLES.

CHARLES: Ha! Sir George Airy! A-birding* thus early? What forbidden game roused you so soon? For no lawful occasion could invite a person of your figure abroad at such unfashionable hours.*

SIR GEORGE: There are some men, Charles, whom Fortune has left free from inquietudes, who are diligently studious to find out ways and means to make themselves uneasy.

CHARLES: Is it possible that anything in nature can ruffle the temper of a man whom the four seasons of the year compliment with as many thousand pounds? Nay, and a father at rest with his ancestors?

SIR GEORGE: Why, there 'tis now! A man that wants money thinks none can be unhappy that has it; but my affairs are in such a whimsical posture that it will require a calculation of my nativity* to find if my gold will relieve me or not.

CHARLES: Ha, ha, ha! Never consult the stars about that; gold has a power beyond them; gold unlocks the midnight councils;[1] gold outdoes the wind, becalms the ship or fills her sails; gold is omnipotent below;* it makes whole armies fight or fly; it buys even souls, and bribes the wretches to betray their country! Then what can thy business be that gold won't serve thee in?

SIR GEORGE: Why, I'm in love.

CHARLES: In love! Ha, ha, ha, ha! In love! Ha, ha, ha! With what, prithee?[2] A cherubim?

SIR GEORGE: No, with a woman.

CHARLES: A woman? Good! Ha, ha, ha! And gold not help thee?

SIR GEORGE: But suppose I'm in love with two—

CHARLES: Aye, if thou'rt in love with two hundred, gold will fetch 'em, I warrant thee, boy. But who are they? Who are they? Come.

SIR GEORGE: One is a lady whose face I never saw, but witty as an angel; the other beautiful as Venus—

CHARLES: And a fool—

SIR GEORGE: For ought I know, for I never spoke to her, but you can inform me. I am charmed by the wit of one, and die for the beauty of the other.

CHARLES: And pray, which are you in quest of now?

SIR GEORGE: I prefer the sensual pleasure. I'm for her I've seen, who is thy father's ward Miranda.

CHARLES: Nay, then, I pity you; for the Jew my father* will no more part with her, and thirty thousand

1 *midnight councils*: Covert or illicit meetings.

2 *prithee*: Please.

pound,* than he would with a guinea to keep me from starving.

SIR GEORGE: Now you see gold can't do everything, Charles.

CHARLES: Yes, for 'tis her gold that bars my father's gate against you.

SIR GEORGE: Why, if he is this avaricious wretch, how camest thou by such a liberal education?

CHARLES: Not a souse[1] out of his pocket, I assure you; I had an uncle who defrayed[2] that charge, but for some little wildnesses of youth, though he made me his heir, left Dad my guardian till I came to years of discretion, which I presume the old gentleman will never think I am; and now he has got the estate into his clutches, it does me no more good than if it lay in Prester John's dominions.*

SIR GEORGE: What, canst thou find no stratagem to redeem it?

CHARLES: I have made many essays[3] to no purpose; though want, the mistress of invention, still tempts me on, yet still the old fox is too cunning for me. I am upon my last project, which, if it fails, then for my last refuge: a brown musket.*

SIR GEORGE: What is't? Can I assist thee?

CHARLES: Not yet – when you can, I have confidence enough in you to ask it.

SIR GEORGE: I am always ready; but what does he intend to do with Miranda? Is she to be sold in private?

---

1 *souse*: A small coin (i.e. 'not a penny').

2 *defrayed*: Paid for.

3 *essays*: Attempts.

Or will he put her up by way of auction, at who bids most? If so, egad,[1] I'm for him: my gold, as you say, shall be subservient to my pleasure.

CHARLES: To deal ingenuously[2] with you, Sir George, I know very little of her, or home; for since my uncle's death, and my return from travel, I have never been well with my father: he thinks my expenses too great, and I his allowance too little; he never sees me, but he quarrels; and to avoid that, I shun his house as much as possible. The report is, he intends to marry her himself.

SIR GEORGE: Can she consent to it?

CHARLES: Yes, faith, so they say; but I tell you, I am wholly ignorant of the matter. Miranda and I are like two violent members of a contrary party: I can scarce allow her beauty, though all the world does; nor she me civility, for that contempt.* I fancy she plays the mother-in-law already, and sets the old gentleman on to do mischief.

SIR GEORGE: Then I've your free consent to get her?

CHARLES: Aye, and my helping hand, if occasion be.

SIR GEORGE: Pugh, yonder's a fool coming this way; let's avoid him.

CHARLES: What, Marplot? No, no, he's my instrument; there's a thousand conveniences in him. He'll lend me his money when he has any, run of my errands and be proud on't; in short, he'll pimp for me, lie for me, drink for me, do anything but fight for me, and that I trust to my own arm for.

---

1 *egad*: An exclamation of surprise or devotion (from 'A God').

2 ingenuously: Straightforwardly.

SIR GEORGE: Nay, then he's to be endured; I never knew his qualifications before.

(*Enter* MARPLOT *with a patch across his face.*)

MARPLOT: Dear Charles, yours. (*Aside:*) Ha! Sir George Airy, the man in the world I have an ambition to be known to! (*To* CHARLES*:*) Give me thy hand, dear boy—

CHARLES: A good assurance!* But hark ye, how came your beautiful countenance clouded in the wrong place?

MARPLOT: I must confess 'tis a little malapropos, but no matter for that; a word with you, Charles. (*Aside, to* CHARLES*:*) Prithee, introduce me to Sir George – he is a man of wit, and I'd give ten guineas to—

CHARLES: When you have 'em, you mean.

MARPLOT: Aye, when I have 'em. Pugh, pox, you cut the thread of my discourse! I would give ten guineas, I say, to be ranked in his acquaintance. Well, 'tis a vast addition to a man's fortune, according to the rout of the world,[1] to be seen in the company of leading men; for then we are all thought to be politicians, or Whigs, or Jacks, or High-Flyers, or Low-Flyers, or Levellers* and so forth; for you must know, we all herd in parties now.

CHARLES: Then a fool for diversion is out of fashion, I find.

MARPLOT: Yes, without[2] it be a mimicking fool, and they are darlings everywhere; but prithee introduce me.

---

1 *the rout of the world*: That is, the lower classes.

2 *without*: Unless.

CHARLES: Well, on condition you'll give us a true account how you came by that mourning[1] nose, I will.

MARPLOT: I'll do it.

CHARLES: Sir George, here's a gentleman has a passionate desire to kiss your hand.

SIR GEORGE: Oh, I honour men of the sword; and I presume this gentleman is lately come from Spain or Portugal, by his scars?*

MARPLOT: No really, Sir George, mine sprung from civil fury. Happening last night into the Groom Porters,* I had a strong inclination to go ten guineas with a sort of a… sort of a… kind of a milksop, as I thought. A pox of the dice he flung out! And my pockets being empty, as Charles knows they sometimes are, he proved a surly North Briton,* and broke my face for my deficiency.

SIR GEORGE: Ha, ha! And did not you draw?

MARPLOT: Draw, sir? Why, I did but lay my hand upon my sword to make a swift retreat, and he roared out, 'Now the Deel a ma sol, sir, gin ye touch yer steel, Ise whip mine through yer wem!'*

SIR GEORGE: Ha, ha, ha!

CHARLES: Ha, ha, ha, ha! Safe was the word – so you walked off, I suppose.

MARPLOT: Yes, for I avoid fighting, purely to be serviceable to my friends, you know—

SIR GEORGE: Your friends are much obliged to you, sir. I hope you'll rank me in that number.

MARPLOT: Sir George, a bow from the side box,* or to be seen in your chariot, binds me ever yours.

---

1 *mourning*: Weeping (running).

SIR GEORGE: Trifles! You may command 'em when you please.

CHARLES: Provided he may command you—

MARPLOT: Me! Why, I live for no other purpose. Sir George, I have the honour to be caressed by most of the reigning toasts of the town. I'll tell 'em you are the finest gentleman—

SIR GEORGE: No, no, prithee let me alone to tell the ladies my parts. Can you convey a letter upon occasion, or deliver a message with an air of business?* Ha!

MARPLOT: With the assurance of a page and the gravity of a statesman.

SIR GEORGE: You know Miranda?

MARPLOT: What, my sister ward? Why, her guardian is mine; we are fellow sufferers. Ah! He is a covetous, cheating, sanctified curmudgeon; that Sir Francis Gripe is a damned old—

CHARLES: I suppose, friend, you forget that he is my father.

MARPLOT: I ask your pardon, Charles, but it is for your sake I hate him. Well, I say, the world is mistaken in him; his outside piety makes him every man's executor, and his inside cunning makes him every heir's jailor. Egad, Charles, I'm half persuaded that thou'rt some ward too, and never of his getting, for thou art as honest a debauchee as ever cuckolded man of quality.

SIR GEORGE: A pleasant fellow.

CHARLES: The dog is diverting sometimes, or there would be no enduring his impertinence; he is pressing to be employed and willing to execute, but some ill fate generally attends all he undertakes, and he oftener spoils an intrigue than helps it.

MARPLOT: If I miscarry 'tis none of my fault; I follow my instructions.

CHARLES: Yes, witness the merchant's wife.

MARPLOT: Pish, pox, that was an accident.

SIR GEORGE: What was it, prithee?

CHARLES: Why, you must know – I had lent a certain merchant my hunting horses, and was to have met his wife in his absence. Sending him along with my groom to make the compliment,* and to deliver a letter to the lady at the same time, what does he do, but gives the husband the letter, and offers her the horses.

MARPLOT: I remember you was even with me, for you denied the letter to be yours, and swore I had a design upon her, which my bones paid for.

CHARLES: Come, Sir George, let's walk round, if you are not engaged, for I have sent my man upon a little earnest business, and have ordered him to bring me the answer into the park.

MARPLOT (*aside*): Business, and I not know it? Egad, I'll watch him.

SIR GEORGE: I must beg your pardon, Charles – I am to meet your father here.

CHARLES: My father!

SIR GEORGE: Aye! And about the oddest bargain perhaps you ever heard of; but I'll not impart till I know the success.

MARPLOT (*aside*): What can his business be with Sir Francis? Now, would I give all the world to know it. Why the devil should not one know every man's concern?

CHARLES: Prosperity to't, whate'er it be. I have private affairs, too; over a bottle we'll compare notes.

MARPLOT (*aside*): Charles knows I love a glass as well as any man; I'll make one.* Shall it be tonight? And I long to know their secrets.

(*Enter* WHISPER.)

WHISPER (*aside to* CHARLES): Sir, sir, Miss Patch says Isabinda's Spanish father* has quite spoilt the plot, and she can't meet you in the park, but he infallibly will go out this afternoon, she says; but I must step again to know the hour.

MARPLOT (*aside*): What did Whisper say now? I shall go stark mad if I'm not let into this secret!

CHARLES (*aside to* WHISPER): Cursed misfortune! Come along with me; my heart feels pleasure at her name. —Sir George, yours; we'll meet at the old place, the usual hour.

SIR GEORGE: Agreed; I think I see Sir Francis yonder. (*Exit.*)

CHARLES: Marplot, you must excuse me, I am engaged.

(*Exeunt* CHARLES *and* WHISPER.)

MARPLOT: Engaged? Egad, I'll engage my life I'll know what your engagement is.

(*Exit* MARPLOT. *Enter* MIRANDA *and* SERVANTS.)

MIRANDA (*coming out of a chair*[1]): Let the chair wait: my servant that dogged[2] Sir George said he was in the park.

(*Exit* SERVANTS*; enter* PATCH.)

Ha! Miss Patch alone? Did not you tell me you had contrived a way to bring Isabinda to the park?

PATCH: Oh, madam, your ladyship can't imagine what a wretched disappointment we have met with! Just as I had fetched a suit of my clothes for a disguise comes my old master into his closet, which is right against her chamber door. This struck us into a terrible fright. At length I put on a grave face, and asked him if he was at leisure for his chocolate, in hopes to draw him out of his hole, but he snapped my nose off – 'No, I shall be busy here this two hours' – at which my poor mistress, seeing no way of escape, ordered me to wait on your ladyship with the sad relation.

MIRANDA: Unhappy Isabinda! Was ever anything so unaccountable as the humour of Sir Jealous Traffick!

PATCH: Oh, madam, it's his living so long in Spain. He vows he'll spend half his estate, but he'll be a Parliament man, on purpose to bring in a bill for women to wear veils, and the other odious Spanish customs. He swears it is the height of impudence to have a woman seen bare-faced, even at church, and scarce believes there's a true-begotten child in the city.

1 *chair*: A sedan chair.

2 *dogged*: Tracked.

MIRANDA: Ha, ha, ha! How the old fool torments himself! Suppose he could introduce his rigid rules – does he think we could not match them in contrivance? No, no, let the tyrant man make what laws he will; if there's a woman under the Government, I warrant she finds a way to break 'em! Is his mind set upon the Spaniard for his son-in-law still?

PATCH: Aye, and he expects him by the next fleet, which drives his daughter to melancholy and despair. But madam, I find you retain the same gay, cheerful spirit you had when I waited on your ladyship. My lady is mighty good-humoured too, and I have found a way to make Sir Jealous believe I am wholly in his interest, when my real design is to serve her; he makes me her jailer, and I set her at liberty.

MIRANDA: I know thy prolific brain would be of singular service to her, or I had not parted with thee to her father.

PATCH: But madam, the report is that you are going to marry your guardian.

MIRANDA: It is necessary such a report should be, Patch.

PATCH: But is it true, madam?

MIRANDA: That's not absolutely necessary.

PATCH: I thought it was only the old strain, coaxing him still for your own, and railing at all the young fellows about town. In my mind now, you are as ill-plagued with your guardian, madam, as my lady is with her father.

MIRANDA: No, I have liberty, wench, that she wants;[1] what would she give now to be in this dishabille[2] in the open air – nay, more, in pursuit of the young fellow she likes! For that's my case, I assure thee.

PATCH: As for that, madam, she's even with you; for though she can't come abroad, we have a way to bring him home in spite of old Argus.*

MIRANDA: Now Patch, your opinion of my choice, for here he comes. Ha! My guardian with him! What can be the meaning of this? I'm sure Sir Francis can't know me in this dress. Let's observe 'em.

(*They withdraw. Enter* SIR FRANCIS GRIPE *and* SIR GEORGE AIRY.)

SIR FRANCIS: Verily, Sir George, thou wilt repent throwing away thy money so, for I tell thee sincerely, Miranda, my charge, does not love a young fellow; they are all vicious,[3] and seldom make good husbands; in sober sadness[4] she cannot abide 'em.

MIRANDA (*peeping*): In sober sadness you are mistaken! What can this mean?

SIR GEORGE: Look ye, Sir Francis, whether she can or cannot abide young fellows is not the business. Will you take the fifty guineas?

SIR FRANCIS: In good truth, I will not, for I knew thy father – he was a hearty wary man, and I cannot

1 *wants*: Lacks.

2 *dishabille*: From the French for 'undressed'; in revealing or informal clothing.

3 *vicious*: i.e. have many vices.

4 *sober sadness*: A figure of speech – i.e. truly.

consent that his son should squander away what he saved to no purpose.

MIRANDA (*peeping*): Now, in the name of wonder, what bargain can he be driving about me for fifty guineas?

PATCH (*peeping, to* MIRANDA): I wish it ben't for the first night's lodging,* madam.

SIR GEORGE: Well, Sir Francis, since you are so conscientious for my father's sake, then permit me the favour gratis.

MIRANDA (*peeping, to* PATCH): The favour!* Oh, my life! I believe 'tis as you said, Patch.

SIR FRANCIS: No, verily, if thou dost not buy thy experience, thou would never be wise; therefore give me a hundred and try fortune.

SIR GEORGE (*aside*): The scruples arose, I find, from the scanty sum. —Let me see… a hundred guineas. (*Takes them out of a purse and chinks them.*) Ha! They have a very pretty sound, and a very pleasing look – but then, Miranda – but if she should be cruel—

MIRANDA (*peeping*): As ten to one I shall!

SIR FRANCIS: Aye, do consider on't. He, he, he, he!

SIR GEORGE: No, I'll do't.

PATCH (*peeping, to* MIRANDA): Do't? What, whether you will or no, madam?

SIR GEORGE: Come to the point! Here's the gold; sum up the conditions.

MIRANDA (*peeping*): Aye, for heaven's sake do, for my expectation is on the rack!

SIR FRANCIS (*pulling out a paper*): Well, at your own peril be it.

SIR GEORGE: Aye, aye, go on.

SIR FRANCIS: *Imprimis*,[1] you are to be admitted into my house in order to move your suit to Miranda for the space of ten minutes, without let[2] or molestation, provided I remain in the same room—

SIR GEORGE: But out of earshot.

SIR FRANCIS: Well, well, I don't desire to hear what you say. Ha, ha, ha! In consideration, I am to have that purse and a hundred guineas.

SIR GEORGE: Take it. (*Gives him the purse.*)

MIRANDA (*peeping*): So, 'tis well it's no worse. I'll fit[3] you both!

SIR GEORGE: And this agreement is to be performed today.

SIR FRANCIS: Aye, aye, the sooner the better. (*Aside:*) Poor fool, how Miranda and I shall laugh at him! —Well, Sir George! Ha, ha, ha! Take the last sound of your guineas, ha, ha, ha! (*Chinks them. Exit.*)

MIRANDA (*peeping*): Sure he does not know I am Miranda.

SIR GEORGE: A very extraordinary bargain I have made, truly. If she should be really in love with this old cuff, now – pshaw! That's morally impossible! But then, what hopes have I to succeed? I never spoke to her.

MIRANDA (*peeping*): Say you so? Then I am safe.

SIR GEORGE: What though my tongue never spoke, my eyes said a thousand things, and my hopes flattered me hers answered 'em. If I'm lucky… if not, 'tis but a hundred guineas thrown away.

(MIRANDA *and* PATCH *come forward.*)

1 *Imprimis*: In the first place (Latin).

2 *let*: Hindrance.

3 *fit*: Match; get even with.

MIRANDA: Upon what, Sir George?

SIR GEORGE: Ha! My Incognita!* Upon a woman, madam.

MIRANDA: They are the worst things you can deal in, and damage the soonest – your very breath destroys 'em, and I fear you'll never see your return, Sir George. Ha, ha!

SIR GEORGE: Were they more brittle than china, and dropped to pieces with a touch, every atom of her I have ventured at, if she is but mistress of thy wit, balances ten times the sum. Prithee let me see thy face.

MIRANDA: By no means – that may spoil your opinion of my sense!

SIR GEORGE: Rather confirm it, madam.

PATCH: So rob the lady of your gallantry, sir?

SIR GEORGE: No, child, a dish of chocolate in the morning never spoils my dinner; the other lady I design a set meal, so there's no danger—

MIRANDA: Matrimony? Ha, ha, ha! What crimes have you committed against the god of love that he should revenge 'em so severely to stamp husband upon your forehead?

SIR GEORGE: For my folly in having so often met you here, without pursuing the laws of nature, and exercising her command. But I resolve, ere we part now, to know who you are, where you live and what kind of flesh and blood your face is. Therefore unmask and don't put me to the trouble of doing it for you!

MIRANDA: My face is the same flesh and blood with my hand, Sir George, which if you'll be so rude to provoke—

SIR GEORGE: You'll apply it to my cheek? The ladies' favours are always welcome, but I must have that cloud withdrawn. (*Taking hold of her:*) Remember you are in the park, child,* and what a terrible thing would it be to lose this pretty white hand.

MIRANDA: And how will it sound in a chocolate-house that Sir George Airy rudely pulled off a lady's mask, when he had given her his honour that he never would, directly or indirectly, endeavour to know her till she gave him leave?

PATCH (*aside*): I wish we were safe out.

SIR GEORGE: But if that lady thinks fit to pursue and meet me at every turn like some troubled spirit, shall I be blamed if I inquire into the reality? I would have nothing dissatisfied in a female shape.

MIRANDA (*aside*): What shall I do?

(*Pause.*)

SIR GEORGE: Aye, prithee consider, for thou shalt find me very much at thy service.

PATCH: Suppose, sir, the lady should be in love with you?

SIR GEORGE: Oh! I'll return the obligation in a moment.

PATCH: And marry her?

SIR GEORGE: Ha, ha, ha! That's not the way to love her, child.

MIRANDA (*aside*): If he discovers me, I shall die! Which way shall I escape? Let me see.

(*Pause.*)

SIR GEORGE: Well, madam?

MIRANDA (*aside*): I have it! —Sir George, 'tis fit you should allow something. If you'll excuse my face, and turn your back – if you look upon me I shall sink, even masked as I am – I will confess why I have engaged you so often, who I am and where I live.

SIR GEORGE: Well, to show you I'm a man of honour I accept the conditions. (*Aside:*) Let me but once know those, and the face won't be long a secret to me.

PATCH (*aside to* MIRANDA): What mean you, madam?

MIRANDA (*aside to* PATCH): To get off.

SIR GEORGE: 'Tis something indecent to turn one's back upon a lady – but you command and I obey. (*Turns his back.*) Come, madam, begin.

MIRANDA (*draws back a little while and speaks*): First, then, it was my unhappy lot to see you at Paris at a ball upon a birthday. Your shape and air charmed my eyes; your wit and complaisance my soul, and from that fatal night I loved you. (*Drawing back.*)

And when you left the place, grief seized me so –
No rest my heart, no sleep my eyes could know.
Last I resolved a hazardous point to try,
And quit the place in search of liberty.

(*Exeunt* MIRANDA *and* PATCH.)

SIR GEORGE: Excellent! (*Aside:*) I hope she's handsome. —Well, now, madam, to the other two things: your name, and where you live. I am a gentleman, and this confession will not be lost upon me. Nay, prithee don't weep, but go on – for I find my heart melts in thy behalf. Speak quickly or I shall turn about. Not yet? (*Aside:*) Poor lady, she expects I should comfort her; and to do her justice, she has said enough to encourage me. (*Turns about.*) —Ha? Gone! The devil, jilted? Why, what a tale has she invented – of Paris, balls and birthdays. Egad, I'd give ten guineas to know who this gypsy[1] is! A curse of my folly – I deserve to lose her; what woman can forgive a man that turns his back?

The bold and resolute, in love and war,
To conquer take the right and swiftest way;
The boldest lover soonest gains the fair,
As courage makes the rudest force obey.
Take no denial, and the dames adore ye;
Closely pursue them and they fall before ye.

(*Exit.*)

THE END OF THE FIRST ACT

1 *gypsy*: A deceitful woman (used as a term of endearment).

ACT II

SCENE I

SIR FRANCIS GRIPE*'s house. Enter* SIR FRANCIS *and* MIRANDA.

SIR FRANCIS: Ha, ha, ha, ha, ha, ha, ha!

MIRANDA: Ha, ha, ha, ha, ha, ha, ha! Oh, I shall die with laughing. The most romantic adventure! Ha, ha! What does the odious young fop mean? A hundred pieces to talk an hour with me? Ho, ha!

SIR FRANCIS: And I'm to be by, too – there's the jest! Adod,[1] if it had been in private, I should not have cared to trust the young dog.

MIRANDA: Indeed and indeed, but you might, Gardee.* Now, methinks there's nobody handsomer than you – so neat, so clean, so good-humoured and so loving.

SIR FRANCIS: Pretty rogue, pretty rogue, and so thou shalt find me, if thou dost prefer thy Gardee before these caperers of the age, thou shalt outshine the Queen's box on an opera night;* thou shalt be the envy of the

---

1 *Adod*: An exclamation (from 'Ah, God').

ring (for I will carry thee to Hyde Park)* and thy equipage[1] shall surpass the – what d'ye call 'em – ambassadors'.

MIRANDA: Nay, I'm sure the discreet part of my sex will envy me more for the inside furniture, when you are in it, than my outside equipage.

SIR FRANCIS: A cunning baggage,[2] a-faith thou art, and a wise one too; and to show thee thou hast not chose amiss, I'll this moment disinherit my son, and settle my whole estate upon thee.

MIRANDA (*aside*): There's an old rogue now. —No, Gardee, I would not have your name be so black in the world – you know my father's will runs that I am not to possess my estate without your consent till I'm five and twenty; you shall only abate the odd seven years, and make me mistress of my estate today, and I'll make you master of my person tomorrow.

SIR FRANCIS: Humph! That may not be safe – no, Chargee, I'll settle it upon thee for pin money;[3] and that will be every bit as well, thou knowest.

MIRANDA (*aside*): Unconscionable old wretch! Bribe me with my own money? Which way shall I get out of his hands?

SIR FRANCIS: Well, what art thou thinking on, my girl, ha? How to banter Sir George?

MIRANDA (*aside*): I must not pretend to banter: he knows my tongue too well. —No, Gardee, I have thought of a way will confound him more than all I could say if I should talk to him seven years.

---

1 *equipage*: Horse and carriage.

2 *baggage*: A good-for-nothing (usually applied to women), seemingly used as a term of endearment.

3 *pin money*: A woman's allowance, a small sum.

SIR FRANCIS: How's that? Oh! I'm transported, I'm ravished, I'm mad!

MIRANDA (*aside*): It would make you mad if you knew all. —I'll not answer him one word, but be dumb to all he says.

SIR FRANCIS: Dumb? Good. Ha, ha, ha! Excellent. Ha, ha! I think I have you now, Sir George! Dumb! He'll go distracted! (*Aside:*) Well, she's the wittiest rogue —Ha, ha, dumb! I can but laugh, ha, ha, to think how damned mad he'll be when he finds he has given his money away for a dumb show. Ha, ha, ha!

MIRANDA: Nay, Gardee, if he did but know my thoughts of him it would make him ten times madder. Ha, ha, ha!

SIR FRANCIS: Aye, so it would, Chargee, to hold him in such derision, to scorn to answer him, to be dumb! Ha, ha, ha, ha!

(*Enter* CHARLES.)

SIR FRANCIS: How now, sirrah,[1] who let you in?

CHARLES: My necessity, sir.

SIR FRANCIS: Sir, your necessities are very impertinent, and ought to have sent[2] before they entered.

CHARLES: Sir, I knew 'twas a word would gain admittance nowhere.

SIR FRANCIS: Then, sirrah, how durst you rudely thrust that upon your father which nobody else would admit?

CHARLES: Sure the name of a son is a sufficient plea? I ask this lady's pardon if I have intruded.

---

1 *sirrah*: A term of address for a man or boy of a lower rank than the speaker; often used to convey contempt.

2 *sent*: It was customary to send in a servant to announce one's visit.

SIR FRANCIS: Aye, aye, ask her pardon, and her blessing, too, if you expect anything from me.

MIRANDA: I believe yours, Sir Francis, in a purse of guineas would be more material. Your son may have business with you – I'll retire.

SIR FRANCIS: I guess his business, but I'll dispatch him; I expect the knight every minute – you'll be in readiness.

MIRANDA: Certainly! (*Aside:*) My expectation is more upon the wing than yours, old gentleman. (*Exit.*)

SIR FRANCIS: Well, sir?

CHARLES: Nay, it is very ill, sir; my circumstances are, I'm sure.

SIR FRANCIS: And what's that to me, sir? Your management should have made them better.

CHARLES: If you please to entrust me with the management of my estate I shall endeavour it, sir.

SIR FRANCIS: What, to set upon a card,[1] and buy a lady's favour at the price of a thousand pieces? To rig out an equipage for a wench, or by your carelessness enrich your steward? To fine for sheriff,* or put up for Parliament-man?

CHARLES: I hope I should not spend it this way; however, I ask only for what my uncle left me – yours you may dispose of as you please, sir.

SIR FRANCIS: That I shall – out of your reach, I assure you, sir. Adod, these young fellows think old men get estates for nothing but them to squander away in dicing, wenching, drinking, dressing and so forth.

CHARLES: I think I was born a gentleman, sir; I'm sure my uncle bred me like one.

1 *set upon a card*: Gamble.

SIR FRANCIS: From which you would infer, sir, that gaming, whoring and the pox, are requisites to a gentleman.

CHARLES (*aside*): Monstrous! When I would ask him only for a support, he falls into these unmannerly reproaches; I must, though against my will, employ invention, and by stratagem relieve myself.

SIR FRANCIS: Sirrah, what is it you mutter, sirrah, ha? (*Holds up his cane.*) I say, you shan't have a groat[1] out of my hands till I please – and maybe I'll never please, and what's that to you?

CHARLES: Nay, to be robbed or have one's throat cut is not much—

SIR FRANCIS: What's that, sirrah? Would ye rob me, or cut my throat, ye rogue?

CHARLES: Heaven forbid, sir – I said no such thing!

SIR FRANCIS: Mercy on me! What a plague it is to have a son of one and twenty who wants to elbow one out of one's life, to edge himself into the estate.

(*Enter* MARPLOT.)

MARPLOT (*aside*): Egad, he's here – I was afraid I had lost him! His secret could not be with his father; his wants are public there. —Guardian, your servant. (*Aside to* CHARLES:) Charles, I know by that sorrowful countenance of thine – the old man's fist is as close as his strongbox,[2] but I'll help thee.

SIR FRANCIS (*aside*): So here's another extravagant coxcomb[3] that will spend his fortune before he comes to't; but he

1 *groat*: A small coin.

2 *strongbox*: A small lockable box, much like a modern portable safe.

3 *coxcomb*: A vain young man; a fool.

shall pay swingeing interest; and so let the fool go on. —Well, what? Does necessity bring you too, sir?

MARPLOT: You have hit it, Guardian – I want a hundred pound.

SIR FRANCIS: For what?

MARPLOT: Pugh, for a hundred things! I can't for my life tell you for what.

CHARLES: Sir, I suppose I have received all the answer I am like to have?

MARPLOT (*aside*): Oh, the devil! If he gets out before me I shall lose him again.

SIR FRANCIS: Aye, sir, and you may be marching as soon as you please – I must see a change in your temper ere you find one in mine.

MARPLOT: Pray, sir, dispatch me; the money, sir – I'm in mighty haste.

SIR FRANCIS (*giving him a note*): Fool, take this and go to the cashier; I shan't be long plagued with thee.

MARPLOT (*aside*): Devil take the cashier, I shall certainly have Charles gone before I come back again. (*Runs out.*)

CHARLES: Well, sir, I take my leave – but remember, you expose an only son to all the miseries of wretched poverty, which too often lays the plan for scenes of mischief.

SIR FRANCIS: Stay, Charles – I have a sudden thought come into my head may prove to thy advantage.

CHARLES (*aside*): Ha, does he relent?

SIR FRANCIS: My Lady Wrinkle, worth forty thousand pound, sets up for a handsome young husband; she praised thee t'other day. Though the matchmakers can get twenty guineas for a sight of her, I can introduce thee for nothing.

CHARLES: My Lady Wrinkle, sir? Why, she has but one eye!

SIR FRANCIS: Then she'll see but half your extravagance, sir.

CHARLES: Condemn me to such a piece of deformity? Toothless, dirty, wry-necked, hunchbacked hag!

SIR FRANCIS: Hunchbacked! So much the better. Then she has a rest for her misfortunes, for thou wilt load her swingeingly. Now, I warrant you think this is no offer of a father* – forty thousand pound is nothing with you.

CHARLES: Yes, sir, I think it is too much – a young, beautiful woman with half the money would be more agreeable. I thank you, sir, but you chose better for yourself, I find.

SIR FRANCIS: Out of my doors, you dog! You pretend to meddle with my marriage, sirrah?

CHARLES: Sir, I obey, but—

SIR FRANCIS: But me no buts! Be gone, sir! Dare to ask me for money again… refuse forty thousand pound! Out of my doors, I say, without reply.

(*Exit* CHARLES. *Enter* SERVANT.)

SERVANT: One Sir George Airy enquires for you, sir.

(*Enter* MARPLOT, *running.*)

MARPLOT: Ha? Gone! Is Charles gone, Guardian?

SIR FRANCIS: Yes, and I desire your wise worship to walk after him.

MARPLOT: Nay, egad, I shall run, I tell you but that! (*Aside:*) Ah, pox of the cashier for detaining me so long. Where the devil shall I find him now? I shall certainly lose this secret. (*Exit, hastily.*)

SIR FRANCIS: What, is the fellow distracted? Desire Sir George to walk up.

(*Exit* SERVANT.)

Now for a trial of skill that will make me happy, and him a fool. Ha, ha, ha! In my mind he looks like an ass already.

(*Enter* SIR GEORGE.)

SIR FRANCIS: Well, Sir George, do ye hold in the same mind? Or would you capitulate? Ha, ha, ha! Look, here are the guineas. (*Chinks them.*) Ha, ha, ha!

SIR GEORGE: Not if they were twice the sum, Sir Francis! Therefore be brief, call in the lady and take your post. (*Aside:*) If she's a woman, and not seduced by witchcraft to this old rogue, I'll make his heart ache; for if she has but one grain of inclination about her, I'll vary a thousand shapes, but find it.

(*Enter* MIRANDA.)

SIR FRANCIS: Agreed. Miranda! There, Sir George, try your fortune. (*Takes out his watch.*)

SIR GEORGE: So from the eastern chambers breaks the sun, dispels the clouds and gilds the vales below. (*Salutes*[1] *her.*)

SIR FRANCIS: Hold, sir! Kissing was not in our agreement.

SIR GEORGE: Oh! That's by way of prologue. Prithee, old Mammon,* to thy post.

1 *salutes*: Kisses, by way of greeting.

SIR FRANCIS: Well, young Timon,* 'tis now four exactly; one hour, remember, is your utmost limit – not a minute more. (*Retires to the bottom of the stage.*)

SIR GEORGE: Madam, whether you will excuse or blame my love, the author of this rash proceeding depends upon your pleasure, as also the life of your admirer. Your sparkling eyes speak a heart susceptible of love; your vivacity a soul too delicate to admit the embraces of decayed mortality.

MIRANDA (*aside*): Oh, that I durst speak…

SIR GEORGE: Shake off this tyrant guardian's yoke, assume yourself and dash his bold aspiring hopes! The deity of his desires is avarice – a heretic in love, and ought to be banished by the queen of beauty. (*Kneeling:*) See, madam, a faithful servant kneels and begs to be admitted in the number of your slaves.

(MIRANDA *gives him her hand to raise him.*)

SIR FRANCIS: I wish I could hear what he says now! (*Running up:*) Hold, hold, hold! No palming[1] – that's contrary to articles—

SIR GEORGE (*laying his hand to his sword*): Death, sir, keep your distance, or I'll write another article in your guts!

SIR FRANCIS (*going back*): A bloody-minded fellow!

SIR GEORGE (*aside*): Not answer me? Perhaps she thinks my address too grave – I'll be more free. —Can you be so unconscionable, madam, to let me say all these fine things to you without one single compliment in return?

1 *palming*: Hand-holding (also trickery could be implied).

View me well: am I not a proper handsome fellow, ha? Can you prefer that old, dry, withered, sapless log of sixty-five to the vigorous, gay, sprightly love of twenty-four? With snoring only he'll awake thee, but I, with ravishing delight, would make thy senses dance in consort with the joyful minutes. (*Aside:*) Ha! Not yet? Sure she is dumb. —Thus would I steal and touch thy beauteous hand (*takes hold of her hand*), till by degrees I reached thy snowy breasts, then ravish kisses thus. (*Embraces her in ecstasy.*)

MIRANDA (*struggling and flinging herself from him; aside*): Oh, heavens! I shall not be able to contain myself.

SIR FRANCIS (*running up with his watch in his hand; aside*): Sure she did not speak to him. —There's three quarters of the hour gone, Sir George. (*Aside:*) Adod, I don't like those close conferences!

SIR GEORGE: More interruptions? You will have it, sir! (*Lays his hand to his sword.*)

SIR FRANCIS (*going back; aside*): No, no, you shan't have her neither.

SIR GEORGE (*aside*): Dumb still? Sure this old dog has enjoined her silence; I'll try another way. —I must conclude, madam, that in compliance to your guardian's humour you refuse to answer me – consider the injustice of his injunction. This single hour cost me a hundred pound – and would you answer me, I could purchase the twenty four so. However, madam, you must give me leave to make the best interpretation I can for my money, and take the indication of your silence for the secret liking of my person. Therefore, madam, I will instruct you how to keep your word inviolate to Sir Francis, and yet answer me to every question. As for example, when I ask anything to which you would reply in the affirmative, gently nod your head – thus (*nods his head*) – and when in the negative thus (*shakes his head*), and in the doubtful a tender sigh, thus (*sighs*).

MIRANDA (*aside*): How every action charms me! But I'll fit him for signs, I warrant him.

SIR FRANCIS (*aside*): Ha, ha, ha, ha! Poor Sir George! Ha, ha, ha, ha!

SIR GEORGE: Was it by his desire that you are dumb, madam, to all that I can say?

(MIRANDA *nods.*)

(*Aside:*) Very well! She's tractable, I find. —And is it possible that you can love him?

(MIRANDA *nods.*)

Miraculous! Pardon the bluntness of my questions, for my time is short. May I not hope to supplant him in your esteem?

(MIRANDA *sighs.*)

(*Aside:*) Good! She answers me as I could wish. —You'll not consent to marry him, then?

(MIRANDA *sighs.*)

(*Aside:*) How? Doubtful in that? Undone again – humph! But that may proceed from his power to keep her out of her estate till twenty five; I'll try that. —Come, madam, I cannot think you hesitate in this affair out of any motive but your fortune – let him keep it till those few years are expired; make me happy with your person, let him enjoy your wealth—

(MIRANDA *holds up her hands.*)

Why, what sign is that now? Nay, nay, madam, except[1] you observe my lesson, I can't understand your meaning.

SIR FRANCIS (*aside*): What a vengeance! Are they talking by signs? Ad,[2] I may be fooled here! —What do you mean, Sir George?

SIR GEORGE: To cut your throat if you dare mutter another syllable!

SIR FRANCIS: Od![3] I wish he were fairly out of my house.

SIR GEORGE: Pray, madam, will you answer me to the purpose?

(MIRANDA *shakes her head, and points to* SIR FRANCIS.)

(*Aside:*) What! Does she mean she won't answer me to the purpose, or is she afraid yon old cuff should understand her signs? Aye, it must be that. —I perceive, madam, you are too apprehensive of the promise you have made to follow my rules; therefore I'll suppose your mind and answer for you – first, for myself, madam, that I am in

1 *except*: Unless.
2 *Ad*: God.
3 *Od*: God.

love with you is an infallible truth. Now for you. (*Turns on her side.*)* Indeed, sir, and may I believe it! (*Turns back.*) As certainly, madam, as that 'tis daylight, or that I die if you persist in silence. Bless me with the music of your voice, and raise my spirits to their proper heaven. Thus low let me entreat; ere I'm obliged to quit this place, grant me some token of a favourable reception to keep my hopes alive. (*Arises hastily, turns of her side.*) Rise, sir, and since my guardian's presence will not allow me privilege of tongue, read that (*offers her a letter*) and rest assured you are not indifferent to me. (*Turns back;* MIRANDA *strikes it down*) Ha! Right woman! But no matter – I'll go on.

SIR FRANCIS: Ha! What's that – a letter? Ha, ha, ha! Thou art baulked.

MIRANDA (*aside*): The best assurance[1] I ever saw!

SIR GEORGE: Ha! A letter? Oh! Let me kiss it with the same raptures that I would do the dear hand that touched it. (*Opens it. Aside:*) Now for a quick fancy and a long extempore. —What's here? (*Reads.*) 'Dear, Sir George, this virgin muse I consecrate to you, which, when it has received the addition of your voice, 'twill charm me into desire of liberty to love, which you, and only you, can fix.' My angel! Oh, you transport me! (*Kisses the letter.*) And see the power of your command. The god of love has set the verse already; the flowing numbers dance into a tune, and I'm inspired with a voice to sing it.

MIRANDA (*aside*): I'm sure thou art inspired with impudence enough.

---

1 *assurance*: Self-confidence.

SIR GEORGE (*sings*):

Great love inspire him;
Say I admire him.
Give me the lover
That can discover
Secret devotion
From silent motion;
Then don't betray me,
But hence convey me.

(*Taking hold of* MIRANDA:) With all my heart, this moment let's retire.

SIR FRANCIS (*coming up hastily*): The hour is expired, sir, and you must take your leave. There, my girl: there's the hundred pound which thou hast won. Go – I'll be with you presently. Ha, ha, ha, ha!

(*Exit* MIRANDA.)

SIR GEORGE: Adsheart,[1] madam, you won't leave me just in the nick, will you?

SIR FRANCIS: Ha, ha, ha! She has nicked[2] you, Sir George, I think! Ha, ha, ha! Have you any more hundred pounds to throw away upon courtship? Ha, ha, ha!

SIR GEORGE: He, he, he, he! A curse of your fleering[3] jests! Yet however ill I succeeded, I'll venture the same wager she does not value thee a spoonful of snuff – nay, more, though you enjoined her silence to me, you'll never make her speak to the purpose with yourself.

---

1 *Adsheart*: An exclamation (from God's heart).

2 *nicked*: Beaten.

3 *fleering*: Impudent laughing.

SIR FRANCIS: Ha, ha, ha! Did not I tell thee thou wouldst repent thy money? Did not I say she hated young fellows? Ha, ha, ha!

SIR GEORGE: And I'm positive she's not in love with age.

SIR FRANCIS: Ha, ha! No matter for that. Ha, ha! She's not taken with your youth, nor your rhetoric to boot. Ha, ha!

SIR GEORGE: Whate'er her reasons are for disliking a[1] me, I am certain she can be taken with nothing about thee.

SIR FRANCIS (*aside*): Ha, ha, ha! How he swells with envy! Poor man, poor man! —Ha, ha! I must beg your pardon, Sir George, Miranda will be impatient to have her share of mirth – verily we shall laugh at thee most egregiously! Ha, ha, ha!

SIR GEORGE: With all my heart, faith, I shall laugh in my turn, too! For if you dare marry her, old Beelzebub,[2] you would be cuckolded most egregiously – remember that, and tremble!

She that to age her beauteous self resigns
Shows witty management for close designs.
Then if thou'rt graced with fair Miranda's bed,
Actaeon's horns she means shall crown thy head.*

(*Exit.*)

SIR FRANCIS: Ha, ha, ha! He is mad.

These fluttering fops imagine they can wind,
Turn and decoy to love all womenkind.

1 *a*: Of.

2 *Beelzebub*: The Devil.

But here's a proof of wisdom in my charge:
Old men are constant, young men live at large.
The frugal hand can bills at sight defray,
When he that lavish is has nought to pay.

(*Exit.*)

SCENE II

SIR JEALOUS TRAFFICK*'s house. Enter* SIR JEALOUS *and* ISABINDA, PATCH *following.*

SIR JEALOUS: What, in the balcony again, notwithstanding my positive commands to the contrary! Why don't you write a bill upon your forehead to show passengers there's something to be let?*

ISABINDA: What harm can there be in a little fresh air, sir?

SIR JEALOUS: Is your constitution so hot, mistress, that it wants cooling, ha? Apply the virtuous Spanish rules: banish your taste and thoughts of flesh, feed upon roots and quench your thirst with water.

ISABINDA: That and a close[1] room would certainly make me die of the vapours.

SIR JEALOUS: No, mistress, 'tis your high-fed, lusty, rambling, rampant ladies that are troubled with the vapours; 'tis your ratifia, persico, cinnamon, citron and spirit of claret* cause such swimming in the brain, that carries many a guinea full-tide to the doctor. But you are not to be bred this way – no galloping abroad, no receiving

---

1 *close*: Shut up, confined.

visits at home, for in our loose country, the women are as dangerous as the men.

PATCH: So I told her, sir; and that it was not decent to be seen in a balcony – but she threatened to slap my chaps, and told me I was her servant, not her governess.

SIR JEALOUS: Did she so? But I'll make her to know that you are her duenna.[1] Oh, that incomparable custom of Spain! Why, here's no depending upon old women in my country, for they are as wanton at eighty as a girl of eighteen; and a man may as safely trust to Asgill's translation* as to his great grandmother's not marrying again.

ISABINDA: Or to the Spanish ladies' veils and duennas for the safeguard of their honour.

SIR JEALOUS: Dare to ridicule the cautious conduct of that wise nation and I'll have you locked up this fortnight, without a peephole.

ISABINDA (*aside*): If we had but the ghostly helps in England which they have in Spain,* I might deceive you if you did. —Sir, 'tis not the restraint but the innate principles secures the reputation and honour of our sex – let me tell you, sir, confinement sharpens the invention, as want of sight strengthens the other senses, and is often more pernicious than the recreation innocent liberty allows.

SIR JEALOUS: Say you so, mistress? Who the devil taught you the art of reasoning? I assure you, they must have a greater faith than I pretend to that can think any woman innocent who requires liberty. Therefore, Patch, to your charge I give her – lock her up till I come back from

1 *duenna*: An older woman acting as governess (especially in Spanish households).

Change.[1] I shall have some sauntering coxcomb, with nothing but a red coat and a feather,* think, by leaping into her arms, to leap into my estate. But I'll prevent them – she shall be only Signeur Barbinetto's.

PATCH: Really, sir, I wish you would employ anybody else in this affair; I lead a life like a dog with obeying your commands. Come, madam, will you please to be locked up?

ISABINDA (*aside*): Aye, to enjoy more freedom than he is aware of.

(*Exeunt* ISABINDA *and* PATCH.)

SIR JEALOUS: I believe this wench is very true to my interest: I am happy I met with her. If I can but keep my daughter from being blown upon[2] till Signeur Barbinetto arrives, who shall marry her as soon as he comes and carry her to Spain as soon as he has married her. She has a pregnant wit, and I'd no more have her an English wife than the Grand Signior's mistress.*

(*Exit* SIR JEALOUS. *Enter* WHISPER.)

WHISPER: So, I see Sir Jealous go out; where shall I find Mrs Patch now?

(*Enter* PATCH.)

PATCH: Oh, Mr Whisper, my Lady saw you out at the window, and ordered me to bid you fly and let your master know she's now alone.

1 *Change*: The Exchange – a place of trade for merchants and bankers.
2 *blown upon*: Sullied; defamed.

WHISPER: Hush, speak softly! I go, go, but harkee, Mrs Patch, shall not you and I have a little confabulation[1] when my master and your lady is engaged?

PATCH: Aye, aye, farewell.

(PATCH *goes in and shuts the door. Re-enter* SIR JEALOUS TRAFFICK, *meeting* WHISPER.)

SIR JEALOUS (*aside*): Sure whilst I was talking with Mr Tradewell I heard my door clap. (*Seeing* WHISPER*:*) Ha! A man lurking about my house! —Who do you want there, sir?

WHISPER: Want? (*Aside:*) Want, a pox, Sir Jealous! What must I say now?

SIR JEALOUS: Aye, want! Have you a letter or message for anybody there? (*Aside:*) O, my conscience, this is some he-bawd![2]

WHISPER: Letter or message, sir?

SIR JEALOUS: Aye, letter or message, sir.

WHISPER: No, not I, sir.

SIR JEALOUS: Sirrah, sirrah, I'll have you set in the stocks if you don't tell me your business immediately.

WHISPER: Nay, sir, my business... is no great matter of business neither; and yet 'tis business of consequence too.

SIR JEALOUS: Sirrah, don't trifle with me.

WHISPER: Trifle, sir? Have you found him, sir?

SIR JEALOUS: Found what, you rascal?

WHISPER: Why, Trifle is the very lapdog my lady lost, sir! I fancied I see him run into this house. I'm glad you

1 *confabulation*: Chat.

2 *he-bawd*: A bawd is a procurer, the women in charge of a brothel.

have him. Sir, my lady will be overjoyed that I have found him!

SIR JEALOUS: Who is your lady friend?

WHISPER: My Lady Love-Puppy, sir.

SIR JEALOUS: My Lady Love-Puppy! Then prithee carry thyself to her, for I know no other whelp that belongs to her; and let me catch ye no more puppy-hunting about my doors, lest I have you pressed into the service,* sirrah!

WHISPER: By no means, sir. Your humble servant. (*Aside:*) I must watch whether he goes or no before I can tell my master. (*Exit.*)

SIR JEALOUS: This fellow has the officious leer of a pimp, and I half suspect a design, but I'll be upon them before they think on me, I warrant 'em. (*Exit.*)

SCENE III

CHARLES' *lodging. Enter* CHARLES *and* MARPLOT.

CHARLES: Honest Marplot, I thank thee for this supply. I expect my lawyer with a thousand pound I have ordered him to take up, and then you shall be repaid.

MARPLOT: Phoh,[1] phoh, no more of that! Here comes Sir George Airy.

(*Enter* SIR GEORGE.)

Cursedly out of humour at his disappointment! See how he looks! Ha, ha, ha!

---

1 *Phoh*: A dismissive exclamation.

SIR GEORGE: Ah, Charles, I am so humbled in my pretensions to plots upon women that I believe I shall never have courage enough to attempt a chambermaid again, I'll tell thee.

CHARLES: Ha, ha! I'll spare you the relation by telling you – impatient to know your business with my father, when I saw you enter, I slipped back into the next room, where I overheard every syllable.

SIR GEORGE: That I said – but I'll be hanged if you heard her answer! But prithee tell me, Charles, is she a fool?

CHARLES: I ne'er suspected her for one; but Marplot can inform you better, if you'll allow him a judge.

MARPLOT: A fool! I'll justify she has more wit than all the rest of her sex put together. Why, she'll rally me till I han't one word to say for myself.

CHARLES: A mighty proof of her wit, truly.

MARPLOT: There must be some trick in't, Sir George. Egad, I'll find it out if it costs me the sum you paid for't.

SIR GEORGE: Do, and command me.

MARPLOT: Enough! Let me alone to trace a secret.

(*Enter* WHISPER, *and speaks aside to his master.*)

(*Aside:*) The devil! Whisper here again? That fellow never speaks out. Is this the same, or a new secret? —Sir George, won't you ask Charles what news Whisper brings?

SIR GEORGE: Not I, sir – I suppose it does not relate to me.

MARPLOT: Lord, lord, how little curiosity some people have! Now, my chief pleasure lies in knowing everybody's business.

SIR GEORGE: I fancy, Charles, thou hast some engagement upon thy hands? I have a little business too. Marplot, if it falls in your way to bring me any intelligence from Miranda, you'll find me at the Thatched House* at six.

MARPLOT: You do me much honour.

CHARLES: You guess right, Sir George. Wish me success.

SIR GEORGE: Better than attended me. Adieu. (*Exit.*)

CHARLES: Marplot, you must excuse me.

MARPLOT: Nay, nay, what need of any excuse amongst friends! I'll go with you.

CHARLES: Indeed, you must not.

MARPLOT: No, then I suppose 'tis a duel, and I will go to secure ye.

CHARLES: Secure me? Why? You won't fight.

MARPLOT: What, then? I can call people to part ye.

CHARLES: Well, but it is no duel – consequently, no danger. Therefore prithee be answered.

MARPLOT: What is't, a mistress, then? Mum.[1] You know I can be silent upon occasion.

CHARLES: I wish you could be civil, too! I tell you, you neither must nor shall go with me. Farewell.

(*Exeunt* CHARLES *and* WHISPER.)

MARPLOT: Why, then, I must and will follow you. (*Exit.*)

THE END OF THE SECOND ACT

1 *Mum*: Silence.

ACT III

SCENE I

SIR JEALOUS TRAFFICK*'s house. Enter* CHARLES.

CHARLES: Well, here's the house which holds the lovely prize quiet and serene; here no noisy footmen throng to tell the world that beauty dwells within; no ceremonious visit makes the lover wait; no rival to give my heart a pang. Who would not scale the window at midnight without fear of the jealous father's pistol, rather than fill up the train of a coquette,[1] where every minute he is jostled out of place? (*Knocks softly.*) Mrs Patch, Mrs Patch!

(*Enter* PATCH.)

PATCH: Oh, are you come, sir? All's safe.
CHARLES: So in – in, then.

(*Exeunt. Enter* MARPLOT.)

---

1 *coquette*: A flirtatious woman.

MARPLOT: There he goes. Who the devil lives here? Except I can find out that, I am as far from knowing his business as ever. Gad, I'll watch – it may be a bawdy house, and he may have his throat cut. If there should be any mischief, I can make oath he went in. Well, Charles, in spite of your endeavour to keep me out of the secret, I may save your life, for ought I know. At that corner I'll plant myself; there I shall see whoever goes in or comes out. Gad, I love discoveries. (*Exit.*)

SCENE II

Scene draws on CHARLES, ISABINDA *and* PATCH.

ISABINDA: Patch, look out sharp – have a care of Dad.
PATCH: I warrant you. (*Exit.*)
ISABINDA: Well, sir, if I may judge your love by your courage, I ought to believe you sincere; for you venture into the lion's den when you come to see me.
CHARLES: If you'd consent whilst the furious beast is abroad, I'd free you from the reach of his paws.
ISABINDA: That would be but to avoid one danger by running into another, like the poor wretches who fly the burning ship and meet their fate in the water. Come, come, Charles, I fear if I consult my reason, confinement and plenty is better than liberty and starving. I know you'd make the frolic pleasing for a little time by saying and doing a world of tender things, but when our small substance is once exhausted and

a thousand requisites for life are wanting, love, who rarely dwells with poverty, would also fail us.

CHARLES: Faith, I fancy not; methinks my heart has laid up a stock will last for life, to back which I have taken a thousand pound upon my uncle's estate.* That surely will support us till one of our fathers relent.

ISABINDA: There's no trusting to that, my friend – I doubt your father will carry his humour to the grave, and mine till he sees me settled in Spain.

CHARLES: And can ye then cruelly resolve to stay till that cursed Don arrives, and suffer that youth, beauty, fire and wit to be sacrificed to the arms of a dull Spaniard, to be immured and forbid the sight of anything that's humane?

ISABINDA: No, when it comes to the extremity, and no stratagem can relieve us, thou shalt list for a soldier, and I'll carry thy knapsack after thee.

CHARLES: Bravely resolved. The world cannot be more savage than our parents, and fortune generally assists the bold; therefore consent now! Why should we put it to a future hazard? Who knows when we shall have another opportunity?

ISABINDA: Oh, you have your ladder of ropes, I suppose, and the closet window stands just where it did; and if you han't forgot to write in characters,[1] Patch will find a way for our assignations. Thus much of the Spanish contrivance my father's severity has taught me, I thank him; though I hate the nation, I admire their management in these affairs.

---

1 *write in characters*: That is, write in code.

(*Enter* PATCH.)

PATCH: Oh, madam, I see my master coming up the street.

CHARLES: Oh, the devil! Would I had my ladder now. I thought you had not expected him till night? Why, why, why, why! What shall I do, madam?

ISABINDA: Oh, for Heaven's sake! Don't go that way, you'll meet him full in the teeth. Oh, unlucky moment!

CHARLES: Adsheart, can you shut me into no cupboard, ram me into no chest, ha?

PATCH: Impossible, sir! He searches every hole in the house.

ISABINDA: Undone for ever! If he sees you, I shall never see you more.

PATCH: I have thought on't. Run you to your chamber, madam; and sir, come you along with me. I'm certain you may easily get down from the balcony.

CHARLES: My life, adieu! Lead on, guide.

(*Exeunt* CHARLES *and* PATCH.)

ISABINDA: Heaven preserve him. (*Exit.*)

SCENE III

Scene changes to the street. Enter SIR JEALOUS, *with* MARPLOT *behind him.*

SIR JEALOUS: I don't know what's the matter, but I have a strong suspicion all is not right within – that fellow's sauntering about my door, and his tale of a puppy, had the face of a lie, methought. By St Jago,[1] if I should find a man in the house, I'd make mincemeat of him!

MARPLOT (*aside*): Ah, poor Charles! Ha? Agad he is old – I fancy I might bully him, and make Charles have an opinion of my courage.

SIR JEALOUS (*feeling for his key*): My own key shall let me in; I'll give them no warning.

MARPLOT (*going up to* SIR JEALOUS): What's that you say, sir?

SIR JEALOUS (*turning quick upon him*): What's that to you, sir?

MARPLOT: Yes, 'tis to me, sir; for the gentleman you threaten is a very honest gentleman. Look to't, for if he comes not as safe out of your house as he went in, I have half a dozen myrmidons[2] hard by shall beat it about your ears.

SIR JEALOUS: Went in? What, is he in, then? Ah! A combination to undo me! I'll myrmidon you, ye dog you! (*Beats* MARPLOT *while he cries:*) Thieves, thieves!

MARPLOT: Murder, murder! I was not in your house, sir.

(*Enter* SERVANT.)

SERVANT: What's the matter, sir?

SIR JEALOUS: The matter, rascals? Have you let a man into my house? But I'll flea[3] him alive! Follow me; I'll not leave a mousehole unsearched – if I find him, by St Jago, I'll equip him for the opera!*

(*Exeunt* SIR JEALOUS *and* SERVANT.)

---

1 *St Jago*: The patron saint of Spain.

2 *myrmidons*: Henchmen, hired thugs.

3 *flea*: Flay.

MARPLOT: A deuce of his cane! There's no trusting to age. What shall I do to relieve Charles? Egad, I'll raise the neighbourhood. Murder! Murder!

(CHARLES *drops down upon him from the balcony.*)

Charles! Faith, I'm glad to see thee safe out – with all my heart.

CHARLES: A pox of your bawling! How the devil came you here?

MARPLOT: Here? Gad, I have done you a piece of service – I told the old thunderbolt that the gentleman that was gone in was—

CHARLES: Was it you that told him, sir? (*Laying hold of him.*) S'death! I could crush thee into atoms.

MARPLOT: What, will you choke me for my kindness?

(*Exit* CHARLES.)

Will my enquiring soul never leave searching into other people's affairs till it gets squeezed out of my body? I dare not follow him now, for, my blood, he's in such a passion! I'll to Miranda – if I can discover ought that may oblige Sir George, it may be a means to reconcile me again to Charles.

(*Exit* MARPLOT. *Enter* SIR JEALOUS *and* SERVANTS.)

SIR JEALOUS: Are you sure you have searched everywhere?

SERVANT: Yes, from the top of the house to the bottom.

SIR JEALOUS: Under the beds, and over the beds?

SERVANT: Yes, and in them, too, but found nobody, sir.
SIR JEALOUS: Why, what could this rogue mean?

(*Enter* ISABINDA *and* PATCH.)

PATCH (*aside to* ISABINDA): Take courage, madam – I saw him safe out.

ISABINDA: Bless me! What's the matter, sir?

SIR JEALOUS: You know best! Pray, where's the man that was here just now?

ISABINDA: What man, sir? I saw none!

PATCH: Nor I, by the trust you repose in me. Do you think I would let a man come within these doors when you were absent?

SIR JEALOUS: Ah, Patch, she may be too cunning for thy honesty! The very scout that he had set to give warning discovered it to me, and threatened me with half a dozen myrmidons – but I think I mauled the villain. These afflictions you draw upon me, mistress!

ISABINDA: Pardon me, sir, 'tis your own ridiculous humour draws you into these vexations and gives every fool pretence to banter you.

SIR JEALOUS: No, 'tis your idle conduct, your coquettish flirting into the balcony... Oh, with what joy shall I resign thee into the arms of Don Diego Barbinetto!

ISABINDA (*aside*): And with what industry shall I avoid him!

SIR JEALOUS: Certainly that rogue had a message from somebody or other, but, being baulked by my coming, popped that sham upon me. (*Addressing the* SERVANTS:) Come along, ye sots, let's see if we can find the dog again. —Patch, lock her up; d'ye hear?

PATCH: Yes, sir.

(*Exeunt* SIR JEALOUS *and* SERVANTS.)

Aye, walk till your heels ache, you'll find nobody, I promise you.

ISABINDA: Who could that scout be which he talks of?

PATCH: Nay, I can't imagine, without[1] it was Whisper.

ISABINDA: Well, dear Patch, let's employ all our thoughts how to escape this horrid Don Diego – my very heart sinks at his terrible name.

PATCH: Fear not, madam, Don Carlo[2] shall be the man, or I'll lose the reputation of contriving, and then what's a chambermaid good for?

ISABINDA: Sayest thou so, my girl? Then:

Let Dad be jealous, multiply his cares,
While love instructs me to avoid the snares;
I'll, spite of all his Spanish caution, show
How much for love a British maid can do.

(*Exeunt.*)

SCENE IV

SIR FRANCIS GRIPE*'s house.* SIR FRANCIS *and* MIRANDA *meeting.*

MIRANDA: Well, Gardee, how did I perform my dumb scene?

---

1 *without*: Unless.

2 *Don Carlo*: That is, Charles (more properly, Carlos in Spanish).

SIR FRANCIS: To admiration – thou dear little rogue, let me buss[1] thee for it! (*Hugging and kissing her.*) Nay, adod, I will, Chargee, so muzzle,[2] and tuzzle,[3] and hug thee; I will, i' faith, I will.

MIRANDA: Nay, Gardee, don't be so lavish;[4] who would ride post[5] when the journey lasts for life?

SIR FRANCIS: Ah wag, ah wag – I'll buss thee again for that.

MIRANDA (*aside*): Phoh! How he stinks of tobacco! What a delicate[6] bedfellow I should have!

SIR FRANCIS: Oh, I'm transported! When, when, my dear, wilt thou convince the world of thy happy day? When shall we marry, ha?

MIRANDA: There's nothing wanting but your consent, Sir Francis.

SIR FRANCIS: My consent! What does my charmer mean?

MIRANDA: Nay, 'tis only a whim, but I'll have everything according to form – therefore, when you sign an authentic paper, drawn up by an able lawyer, that I have your leave to marry, the next day makes me yours, Gardee.

SIR FRANCIS: Ha, ha, ha! A whim indeed! Why, is it not demonstration I give my leave when I marry thee?

MIRANDA: Not for your reputation, Gardee; the malicious world will be apt to say you tricked me into marriage, and so take the merit from my choice. Now, I will have the act my own, to let the idle fops see how much I prefer a man loaded with years and wisdom.

---

1 *buss*: Kiss.

2 *muzzle*: Caress with the mouth.

3 *tuzzle*: A form of 'tussle' – to struggle with, seemingly romantically.

4 *lavish*: Reckless, unrestrained.

5 *post*: With great speed.

6 *delicate*: That is, pleasing to the senses.

SIR FRANCIS: Humph! Prithee leave out years, Chargee – I'm not so old as thou shalt find! Adod, I'm young – there's a caper for ye! (*Jumps.*)

MIRANDA: Oh, never excuse[1] it – why, I like you the better for being old! But I shall suspect you don't love me if you refuse me this formality.

SIR FRANCIS: Not love thee, Chargee! Adod, I do love thee – better than… than… than… better than… what shall I say? Egad, better than money! I' faith I do.

MIRANDA (*aside*): That's false, I'm sure. —To prove it, do this, then.

SIR FRANCIS: Well, I will do it, Chargee, provided I bring a licence at the same time.

MIRANDA: Aye, and a parson too, if you please. Ha, ha, ha! I can't help laughing to think how all the young coxcombs about town will be mortified when they hear of our marriage!

SIR FRANCIS: So they will, so they will. Ha, ha, ha!

MIRANDA: Well, I fancy I shall be so happy with my Gardee!

SIR FRANCIS: If wearing pearls and jewels, or eating gold, as the old saying is, can make thee happy, thou shalt be so, my sweetest, my lovely, my charming, my… Verily, I know not what to call thee.

MIRANDA: You must know, Gardee, that I am so eager to have this business concluded that I have employed my woman's brother, who is a lawyer in the Temple, to settle matters just to your liking. You are to give your consent to my marriage, which is to yourself, you know. But mum: you must take no notice of that. So then I

1 *excuse*: Apologise for.

will – that is, with your leave – put my writings[1] into his hands; then tomorrow we come slap upon them with a wedding that nobody thought on, by which you seize me and my estate, and I suppose make a bonfire of your own act and deed.*

SIR FRANCIS: Nay, but Chargee, if—

MIRANDA: Nay, Gardee, no ifs! Have I refused three northern lords, two British peers and half a score knights to have you put in your ifs?

SIR FRANCIS: So thou hast indeed, and I will trust to thy management. Od, I'm all of a fire.

MIRANDA (*aside*): 'Tis a wonder the dry stubble does not blaze.

(*Enter* MARPLOT.)

SIR FRANCIS: How now! Who sent for you, sir? What, 'sthe hundred pound gone already?

MARPLOT: No, sir, I don't want money now.

SIR FRANCIS: No? That's a miracle! But there's one thing you want, I'm sure.

MARPLOT: Aye? What's that, Guardian?

SIR FRANCIS: Manners! What, had I no servants without?[2]

MARPLOT: None that could do my business, Guardian, which is at present with this lady.

MIRANDA: With me, Mr Marplot? What is it, I beseech you?

SIR FRANCIS: Aye, sir, what is it? Anything that relates to her may be delivered to me.

MARPLOT: I deny that.

---

1 *writings*: Affairs; more literally, likely, legal and financial documents.

2 *without*: Outside.

MIRANDA: That's more than I do, sir.

MARPLOT: Indeed, madam? Why, then to proceed: fame says[1] that you and my most conscionable guardian here designed, contrived, plotted and agreed to chouse[2] a very civil, honourable, honest gentleman out of a hundred pound.

MIRANDA: That I contrived it!

MARPLOT: Aye, you – you said never a word against it; so far you are guilty.

SIR FRANCIS: Pray tell that civil, honourable, honest gentleman that if he has any more such sums to fool away, they shall be received like the last. Ha, ha, ha, ha! Choused, quotha![3] But hark ye, let him know at the same time that if he dare to report I tricked him of it, I shall recommend a lawyer to him shall show him a trick for twice as much! D'ye hear? Tell him that.

MARPLOT: So, and this is the way you use a gentleman, and my friend?

MIRANDA: Is the wretch thy friend?

MARPLOT: The wretch! Look ye, madam, don't call names – egad, I won't take it.

MIRANDA: Why, you won't beat me, will you? Ha, ha!

MARPLOT: I don't know whether I will or no.

SIR FRANCIS: Sir, I shall make a servant show you out at the window if you are saucy.[4]

MARPLOT: I am your most humble servant, Guardian. I design to go out the same way I came in. I would only

1 *Fame says*: Rumour has it.

2 *chouse*: Swindle.

3 *quotha*: He said.

4 *saucy*: Impertinent, particularly towards superiors.

ask this lady if she does not think in her soul Sir George Airy is not a fine gentleman.

MIRANDA: He dresses well.

SIR FRANCIS: Which is chiefly owing to his tailor and valet de chambre.[1]

MIRANDA: And if you allow that a proof of his being a fine gentleman, he is so.

MARPLOT: The judicious part of the world allow him wit, courage, gallantry and management – though I think he forfeited that character when he flung away a hundred pound upon your dumb ladyship.

SIR FRANCIS: Does that gall him? Ha, ha, ha!

MIRANDA: So, Sir George, remaining in deep discontent, has sent you, his trusty squire, to utter his complaint? Ha, ha, ha!

MARPLOT: Yes, madam, and you, like a cruel, hard-hearted Jew,* value it no more than I would your ladyship were I Sir George, you, you, you—

MIRANDA: Oh, don't call names. I know you love to be employed, and I'll oblige you: and you shall carry him a message from me.

MARPLOT: According[2] as I like it. What is it?

MIRANDA: Nay, a kind one, you may be sure. First tell him I have chose this gentleman (*clapping her hand into* SIR FRANCIS') to have and to hold, and so forth.

SIR FRANCIS (*aside*): Oh, the dear rogue, how I dote on her!

MIRANDA: And advise his impertinence to trouble me no more, for I prefer Sir Francis for a husband before all the fops in the universe.

---

1 *valet de chambre*: A gentleman's man, his personal attendant.

2 *According*: As long as.

MARPLOT: Oh lord, oh lord! She's bewitched, that's certain; here's a husband for eighteen!* (*Turning* SIR FRANCIS *about:*) Here's a shape – here's bones rattling in a leather bag! Here's buckram,[1] and canvas, to scrub you to repentance.

SIR FRANCIS: Sirrah, my cane shall teach you repentance presently.

MARPLOT: No, faith, I have felt its twin brother from just such a withered hand too lately.

MIRANDA: One thing more: advise him to keep from the garden gate on the left hand; for if he dares to saunter there about the hour of eight, as he used to do, he shall be saluted with a pistol or a blunderbuss.[2]

SIR FRANCIS: Oh, monstrous! Why, Chargee, did he use to come to the garden gate?

MIRANDA: The gardener described just such another man that always watched his coming out and fain would have bribed him for his entrance. Tell him he shall find a warm reception if he comes this night!

MARPLOT: Pistols and blunderbusses! Egad, a warm reception indeed – I shall take care to inform him of your kindness, and advise him to keep further off.

MIRANDA (*aside*): I hope he will understand my meaning better than to follow your advice.

SIR FRANCIS: Thou hast signed, sealed and ta'en possession of my heart for ever, Chargee! Ha, ha, ha! And for you, Mr Saucebox, let me have no more of your messages if ever you design to inherit your estate, gentleman.

---

1 *buckram*: Coarse fabric used in bookbinding.

2 *blunderbuss*: A historical short, large-bore gun.

MARPLOT: Why, there 'tis now. Sure I shall be out of your clutches one day. Well, Guardian, I say no more; but if you be not as errant a cuckold as e'er drove bargain upon the Exchange or paid attendance to a Court, I am the son of a whetstone.* And so, your humble servant. (*Exit.*)

MIRANDA (*calling after him*): Don't forget the message! Ha, ha!

SIR FRANCIS: I am so provoked! 'Tis well he's gone.

MIRANDA: Oh, mind him not, Gardee, but let's sign articles, and then—

SIR FRANCIS: And then— Adod, I believe I am metamorphosed! (*Kissing and hugging her:*) My pulse beats high and my blood boils, methinks!

MIRANDA: Oh fie, Gardee, be not so violent – consider the market lasts all the year.* Well, I'll in and see if the lawyer be come. You'll follow?

SIR FRANCIS: Aye, to the world's end, my dear.

(*Exit* MIRANDA.)

Well, Frank, thou art a lucky fellow in thy old age to have such a delicate morsel – and thirty thousand pound – in love with thee! I shall be the envy of bachelors, the glory of married men and the wonder of the town. Some guardians would be glad to compound for[1] part of the estate at dispatching an heiress, but I engross the whole: *O! Mihi praeteritos referet si Jupiter Annos.** (*Exit.*)

1 *to compound for*: To accept; to bargain for.

SCENE V

Scene changes to a tavern; discovers SIR GEORGE *and* CHARLES *with wine before them, and* WHISPER *waiting*

SIR GEORGE: Nay, prithee don't be grave, Charles. Misfortunes will happen. Ha, ha, ha! 'Tis some comfort to have a companion in our sufferings.

CHARLES: I am only apprehensive for Isabinda; her father's humour is implacable, and how far his jealousy may transport him to her undoing shocks my soul to think.

SIR GEORGE: But since you escaped undiscovered by him, his rage will quickly lash into a calm, never fear it.

CHARLES: But who knows what that unlucky dog Marplot told him! Nor can I imagine what brought him thither. That fellow is ever doing mischief – and yet, to give him his due, he never designs it. This is some blundering adventure, wherein he thought to show his friendship, as he calls it. A curse on him!

SIR GEORGE: Then you must forgive him. What said he?

CHARLES: Said? Nay, I had more mind to cut his throat than hear his excuses.

SIR GEORGE: Where is he?

WHISPER: Sir, I saw him go into Sir Francis Gripe's just now.

CHARLES: Oh! Then he is upon your business, Sir George. A thousand to one but he makes some mistake there too.

SIR GEORGE: Impossible, without he huffs[1] the lady and makes love to Sir Francis.

---

1 *huffs*: Insults; is rude to.

(*Enter* DRAWER.)

DRAWER: Mr Marplot is below, gentlemen, and desires to know if he may have leave to wait upon ye.

CHARLES: How civil the rogue is when he has done a fault!

SIR GEORGE: Ho! Desire him to walk up.

(*Exit* DRAWER.)

Prithee, Charles, throw off this chagrin, and be good company.

CHARLES: Nay, hang him, I'm not angry with him. Whisper, fetch me pen, ink and paper.

WHISPER: Yes, sir.

(*Exit* WHISPER. *Enter* MARPLOT.)

CHARLES: Do but mark his sheepish look, Sir George.

MARPLOT: Dear Charles, don't o'erwhelm a man already under insupportable affliction. I'm sure I always intend to serve my friends; but if my malicious stars deny the happiness, is the fault mine?

SIR GEORGE: Never mind him, Mr Marplot, he is eat up with spleen.[1] But tell me, what says Miranda?

MARPLOT: Says? Nay, we are all undone there too.

CHARLES: I told you so! Nothing prospers that he undertakes.

MARPLOT: Why can I help her having chose your father for better for worse?

---

1 *spleen*: Melancholy.

CHARLES: So, there's another of Fortune's strokes! I suppose I shall be edged out of my estate, with twins every year, let who will get[1] 'em.

SIR GEORGE: What, is the woman really possessed?

MARPLOT: Yes, with the spirit of contradiction – she railed at you most prodigiously.

SIR GEORGE: That's no ill sign.

(*Enter* WHISPER, *with pen, ink and paper.*)

MARPLOT: You'd say it was no good sign if you knew all.

SIR GEORGE: Why, prithee?

MARPLOT: Harkee, Sir George, Let me warn you, pursue your old haunt no more – it may be dangerous.

(CHARLES *sits down to write.*)

SIR GEORGE: My old haunt? What d'you mean?

MARPLOT: Why, in short, then, since you will have it, Miranda vows if you dare approach the garden gate at eight o'clock, as you used, you shall be saluted with a blunderbuss, sir. These were her words – nay, she bid me tell you so, too.

SIR GEORGE: Ha! The garden gate at eight, as I used to do! There must be a meaning in this. Is there such a gate, Charles?

CHARLES: Yes, yes – it opens into the park. I suppose her ladyship has made many a scamper through it.

SIR GEORGE: It must be an assignation then. Ha! My heart springs with joy! 'Tis a propitious omen. My dear

1 *get*: Beget.

Marplot, let me embrace thee – thou art my friend, my better angel—

MARPLOT: What do you mean, Sir George?

SIR GEORGE: No matter what I mean. Here – take a bumper[1] to the garden gate, ye dear rogue, you.

MARPLOT: You have reason to be transported, Sir George. I have saved your life.

SIR GEORGE: My life! Thou hast saved my soul, man. Charles, if thou dost not pledge this health,[2] may'st thou never taste the joys of love!

CHARLES: Whisper, be sure you take care how you deliver this. (*Gives him the letter.*) Bring me the answer to my lodgings.

WHISPER: I warrant you, sir. (*Exit.*)

MARPLOT (*aside*): Whither does that letter go? Now dare I not ask for my blood.

CHARLES: Now I'm for you.

SIR GEORGE: To the garden gate at the hour of eight, Charles – along, huzza!

CHARLES: I begin to conceive you.

MARPLOT: That's more than I do. Egad, to the garden gate, huzza! (*Drinks.*) But I hope you design to keep far enough off on't, Sir George.

SIR GEORGE: Aye, aye, never fear that – she shall see I despise her frowns. Let her use her blunderbuss against the next fool; she shan't reach me with the smoke, I warrant her. Ha, ha, ha!

MARPLOT: Ah, Charles, if you could receive a disappointment thus *en cavalier*,* one should have some comfort in being beat for you.

---

1 *bumper*: A brimming glass; i.e. 'Cheers to…'

2 *pledge this health*: Join in raising a glass.

CHARLES (*to* SIR GEORGE): The fool comprehends nothing.

SIR GEORGE (*to* CHARLES): Nor would I have him! Prithee take him along with thee.

CHARLES: Enough! Marplot, you shall go home with me.

MARPLOT (*aside*): I'm glad I'm well with him, however. —Sir George, yours. (*Aside:*) Egad, Charles asking me to go home with him gives me a shrewd suspicion there's more in the garden gate than I comprehend. Faith, I'll give him the drop,[1] and away to Guardian's and find it out.

SIR GEORGE: I kiss both your hands.

(*Exeunt* CHARLES *and* MARPLOT.)

And now for the garden gate.

It's beauty gives the assignation there,
And love too powerful grows t'admit of fear.

(*Exit.*)

THE END OF THE THIRD ACT

1 *the drop*: The slip.

ACT IV

SCENE I

The outside of SIR JEALOUS TRAFFICK*'s house,* PATCH *peeping out of door. Enter* WHISPER.

WHISPER: Ha! Mrs Patch, this is a lucky minute to find you so readily – my master dies with impatience.

PATCH: My lady imagined so, and by her orders I have been scouting this hour in search of you to inform you that Sir Jealous has invited some friends to supper with him tonight, which gives an opportunity to your master to make use of his ladder of ropes. The closet window shall be open, and Isabinda ready to receive him; bid him come immediately.

WHISPER: Excellent. He'll not disappoint, I warrant him. But hold – I have a letter here, which I'm to carry an answer of. I can't think what language the direction is.

PATCH: Phoh, 'tis no language, but a character which the lovers invented to avert discovery. Ha, I hear my old master coming downstairs; it is impossible you should have an answer. Away, and bid him come himself for that – begone! We are ruined if you're seen, for he has doubled his care since the last accident.

WHISPER: I go, I go! (*Exit.*)

PATCH: There, go thou into my pocket. (*Puts it besides,* and it falls down.*) Now I'll up the back stairs, lest I meet him. Well, a dexterous chambermaid is the ladies' best utensil, I say.

(*Exit* PATCH. *Enter* SIR JEALOUS *with a letter in his hand.*)

SIR JEALOUS: So, this is some comfort. This tells me that Seignior Don Diego Barbinetto is safely arrived. He shall marry my daughter the minute he comes. Ha! What's here? (*Takes up the letter* PATCH *dropped.*) A letter? I don't know what to make of the superscription.[1] I'll see what's within side. (*Opens it.*) Humph... 'tis Hebrew, I think. What can this mean? There must be some trick in it – this was certainly designed for my daughter, but I don't know that she can speak any language but her mother tongue. No matter for that – this may be one of Love's hieroglyphics, and I fancy I saw Patch's tail sweep by. That wench may be a slut, and, instead of guarding my honour, betray it! I'll find it out, I'm resolved.

(*Enter* SERVANT.)

Who's there? What answer did you bring from the gentlemen I sent you to invite?

1 *superscription*: The writing on the outside.

SERVANT: That they'd all wait of[1] you, sir, as I told you before, but I suppose you forget, sir?

SIR JEALOUS: Did I so, sir? But I shan't forget to break your head if any of 'em come, sir.

SERVANT: Come, sir? Why, did not you send me to desire their company, sir?

SIR JEALOUS: But I send you now to desire their absence. Say I have something extraordinary fallen out, which calls me abroad, contrary to expectation, and ask their pardon, and, d'ye hear, send the butler to me.

SERVANT: Yes, sir.

(*Exit* SERVANT. *Enter* BUTLER.)

SIR JEALOUS: If this paper has a meaning I'll find it. Lay the cloth[2] in my daughter's chamber, and bid the cook send supper thither presently.

BUTLER: Yes, sir. (*Aside:*) Heyday,[3] what's the matter now? (*Exit.*)

SIR JEALOUS: He wants the eyes of Argus* that has a young handsome daughter in this town, but my comfort is I shall not be troubled long with her. He that pretends to rule a girl once in her teens had better be at sea in a storm, and would be in less danger.

For let him do, or counsel, all he can,
She thinks and dreams of nothing else but man.

(*Exit.*)

1 *wait of*: Wait on.

2 *cloth*: Tablecloth.

3 *Heyday*: An exclamation of surprise.

SCENE II

ISABINDA*'s chamber,* ISABINDA *and* PATCH.

ISABINDA: Are you sure nobody saw you speak to Whisper?

PATCH: Yes, very sure madam, but I heard Sir Jealous coming downstairs, so I clapped this letter into my pocket. (*Feels for the letter.*)

ISABINDA: A letter! Give it me quickly.

PATCH (*searching still*): Bless me! What's become on't? I'm sure I put it—

ISABINDA: Is it possible thou couldst be so careless? Oh! I'm undone for ever if it be lost.

PATCH: I must have dropped it upon the stairs. But why are you so much alarmed? If the worst happens nobody can read it, madam, nor find out whom it was designed for.

ISABINDA: If it falls into my father's hands the very figure of a letter will produce ill consequences. Run and look for it upon the stairs this moment.

PATCH: Nay, I'm sure it can be nowhere else.

(*As she's going out of the door, meets the* BUTLER.)

How now, what do you want?

BUTLER: My master ordered me to lay the cloth here for his supper.

ISABINDA (*aside*): Ruined past redemption!

PATCH: You mistake, sure? (*To* ISABINDA:) What shall we do?

ISABINDA: I thought he expected company tonight. (*Aside:*) Oh, poor Charles! Oh, unfortunate Isabinda.

BUTLER: I thought so too, madam, but I suppose he has altered his mind. (*Lays the cloth, and exits.*)

ISABINDA: The letter is the cause. This heedless action has undone me! Fly and fasten the closet window, which will give Charles notice to retire.

(*Enter* SIR JEALOUS.)

Ha, my father! Oh, confusion!

SIR JEALOUS: Hold, hold, Patch. Whither are you going? I'll have nobody stir out of the room till after supper.

PATCH: Sir, I was only going to reach your easy chair. (*Aside:*) Oh! Wretched accident!

SIR JEALOUS: I'll have nobody stir out of the room. I don't want my easy chair.

ISABINDA (*aside*): What will be the event[1] of this?

SIR JEALOUS: Hark ye, daughter, do you know this hand?

ISABINDA (*aside*): As I suspected! —Hand, do you call it, sir? 'Tis some schoolboy's scrawl.

PATCH (*aside*): O, Invention, thou chambermaid's best friend, assist me.

SIR JEALOUS: Are you sure you don't understand it?

(PATCH *feels in her bosom, and shakes her coats.*[2])

---

1 *event*: Result.

2 *coats*: Petticoats.

ISABINDA: Do you understand it, sir?

SIR JEALOUS: I wish I did.

ISABINDA (*aside*): Thank Heaven you do not. —Then I know no more of it than you do, indeed, sir.

PATCH: Oh lord, oh lord, what have you done, sir? Why, the paper is mine! I dropped it out of my bosom. (*Snatching it from him.*)

SIR JEALOUS: Ha! Yours, mistress?

ISABINDA (*aside*): What does she mean by owning it?

PATCH: Yes, sir, it is.

SIR JEALOUS: What is it? Speak!

PATCH: Why, sir, it is a charm for the toothache – I have worn it this seven year. 'Twas given me by an angel, for ought I know, when I was raving with the pain, for nobody knew from whence he came, nor whither he went; he charged me never to open it, lest some dire vengeance befall me, and Heaven knows what will be the event. Oh! Cruel misfortune that I should drop it, and you should open it! If you had not opened it—

ISABINDA (*aside*): Excellent wench.

SIR JEALOUS: Pox of your charms and whims for me! If that be all, 'tis well enough. There, there, burn it, and I warrant you no vengeance will follow.

PATCH (*aside*): So all's right again thus far.

ISABINDA (*aside*): I would not lose Patch for the world – I'll take courage a little. —Is this usage for your daughter, sir? Must my virtue and conduct be suspected? For every trifle you immure[1] me like some

---

1 *immure*: Lock up, confine.

dire offender here, and deny me all recreations which my sex enjoy and the custom of the country and modesty allow. Yet, not content with that, you make my confinement more intolerable by your mistrusts and jealousies. Would I were dead, so I were free from this! (*Weeps.*)

SIR JEALOUS: Tomorrow rids you of this tiresome load – Don Diego Barbinetto will be here, and then my care ends and his begins.

ISABINDA (*aside*): Is he come, then! Oh, how shall I avoid this hated marriage?

(*Enter* SERVANTS *with supper.*)

SIR JEALOUS: Come, will you sit down?

ISABINDA: I can't eat, sir.

PATCH (*aside*): No, I dare swear he has given her supper enough. I wish I could get into the closet.

SIR JEALOUS: Well, if you can't eat, then give me a song whilst I do.

ISABINDA: I have such a cold I can scarce speak, sir, much less sing. (*Aside:*) How shall I prevent Charles coming in?

SIR JEALOUS: I hope you have the use of your fingers, madam. Play a tune upon your spinet,[1] whilst your woman sings me a song.

PATCH (*aside*): I'm as much out of tune as my lady, if he knew all.

ISABINDA: I shall make excellent music. (*Sits down to play.*)

---

1 *spinet*: An instrument like a small harpsichord.

PATCH: Really, sir, I'm so frighted about your opening this charm that I can't remember one song.

SIR JEALOUS: Pish, hang your charm! Come, come, sing anything.

PATCH (*aside*): Yes, I'm likely to sing,[1] truly. —Humph, humph...* Bless me, sir, I cannot raise my voice, my heart pants so.

SIR JEALOUS: Why? (*To* ISABINDA:) What, does your heart pant so that you can't play, neither? Pray, what key are you in, ha?

PATCH (*aside*): Ah, would the key was turned of you once.*

SIR JEALOUS: Why don't you sing, I say?

PATCH: When madam has put her spinet in tune, sir. Humph, humph.

ISABINDA (*rising*): I cannot play, sir, whatever ails me.

SIR JEALOUS: Zounds![2] Sit down and play me a tune, or I'll break the spinet about your ears.

ISABINDA (*aside*): What will become of me? (*Sits down and plays.*)

SIR JEALOUS (*to* PATCH): Come, mistress.

PATCH: Yes, sir. (*Sings, but horribly out of tune.*)

SIR JEALOUS: Hey, hey! Why, you are atop of the house, and you are down in the cellar.* What is the meaning of this? Is it on purpose to cross me, ha?

PATCH: Pray, madam, take it a little lower, I cannot reach that note... nor any note, I fear.

ISABINDA: Well, begin. (*Aside to* PATCH:) Oh! Patch, we shall be discovered!

---

1 *sing*: Sing out, warn.

2 *Zounds*: Exclamation of surprise or frustration (from 'God's wounds').

PATCH (*aside to* ISABINDA): I sink with the apprehension, madam. Humph, humph. (*Sings:*)

'Tis thus the bright celestial Court above
Beguiles the hours with music and with love.

(CHARLES *pulls open the closet door.*)

CHARLES: Music and singing?

(*The women shriek.*)

Death! Her father there? Then I must fly!

(*Exit* CHARLES *into the closet.* SIR JEALOUS *rises up hastily, seeing* CHARLES *slip back into the closet.*)

SIR JEALOUS: Hell and furies, a man in the closet!

PATCH: Ah! A ghost, a ghost! (*Aside:*) He must not enter the closet!

(ISABINDA *throws herself down before the closet door as in a sound.*[1])

SIR JEALOUS: The devil! I'll make a ghost of him, I warrant you! (*Strives to get by.*)

PATCH: Oh, hold, sir, have a care! You'll tread upon my lady! Who waits there?* Bring some water. Oh! This comes of your opening the charm! Oh, oh, oh, oh. (*Weeps aloud.*)

---

1 *sound*: Swoon.

SIR JEALOUS: I'll charm you, housewife! Here lies the charm* that conjured this fellow in, I'm sure on't. Come out, you rascal, do so! Zounds, take her from the door, or I'll spurn her from it, and break your neck down stairs.

ISABINDA: Oh, oh, where am I? (*Aside to* PATCH:) He's gone – I heard him leap down.

PATCH (*aside to* ISABINDA): Nay, then let him enter. — Here, here, madam, smell to this.* Come, give me your hand. Come nearer to the window – the air will do you good.

SIR JEALOUS (*aside*): I would she were in her grave. — Where are you, sirrah, villain, robber of my honour? I'll pull you out of your nest! (*Goes into the closet.*)

PATCH (*aside*): You'll be mistaken, old gentleman, the bird is flown.

ISABINDA (*aside*): I'm glad I have 'scaped so well. I was almost dead in earnest with the fright.

(*Re-enter* SIR JEALOUS *out of the closet.*)

SIR JEALOUS: Whoever the dog were, he has escaped out of the window, for the sash is up. But though he is got out of my reach, you are not. And first, Mrs Pander,[1] with your charms for toothache, get out of my house! Go, troop.[2] Yet hold, stay – I'll see you out of my doors myself, but I'll secure your charge ere I go.

ISABINDA: What do you mean, sir? Was she not a creature of your own providing?

---

1 *Pander*: A go-between in secret love affairs.

2 *troop*: Be off with you.

SIR JEALOUS: She was of the Devil's providing for ought I know.

PATCH: What have I done, sir to merit your displeasure?

SIR JEALOUS: I don't know which of you have done it, but you shall both suffer for it till I can discover whose guilt it is. (*To* ISABINDA:) Go, get in there – I'll move you from this side of the house. (*Pushes* ISABINDA *in at the other door and locks it; puts the key in his pocket.*) I'll keep the key myself; I'll try what ghost will get into that room. And now, forsooth (*to* PATCH:) I'll wait on you downstairs.

PATCH: Ah, my poor lady! Downstairs, sir? But I won't go out, sir, till I have looked up my clothes.

SIR JEALOUS: If thou wert as naked as thou wert born, thou shouldst not stay to put on a smock. Come along, I say. When your mistress is married you shall have your rags, and everything that belongs to you, but till then—

PATCH: Oh! Barbarous usage for nothing!

(*Exeunt,* SIR JEALOUS *pulling* PATCH *out.*)

SCENE III

Re-enter at the lower door.

SIR JEALOUS: There! Go, and, come no more within sight of my habitation these three days, I charge you. (*Exit. and slaps the door after him.*)

PATCH: Did ever anybody see such an old monster!

(*Enter* CHARLES.)

PATCH: Oh, Mr Charles! Your affairs and mine are in an ill posture.

CHARLES: I am immured to the frowns of fortune:* but what has befall'n thee?

PATCH: Sir Jealous, whose suspicious nature's always on the watch – nay, even whilst one eye sleeps, the other keeps sentinel – upon sight of you flew into such a violent passion that I could find no stratagem to appease him, but, in spite of all arguments, locked his daughter into his own apartment and turned me out of doors.

CHARLES: Ha! Oh, Isabinda!

PATCH: And swears she shall neither see sun nor moon till she is Don Diego Barbinetto's wife, who arrived last night, and is expected with impatience.

CHARLES: He dies! Yes, by all the wrongs of love he shall – here will I plant myself, and through my breast he shall make his passage if he enters.

PATCH: A most heroic resolution. There might be ways found out more to your advantage. Policy is often preferred to open force.

CHARLES: I apprehend[1] you not.

PATCH: What think you of personating this Spaniard, imposing upon the father and marrying your mistress by his own consent?

CHARLES: Say'st thou so, my angel? Oh, could that be done, my life to come would be too short to recompense thee! But how can I do that, when I neither

1 *apprehend*: Understand.

know what ship he came in, nor from what part of Spain, who recommends him, nor how attended?*

PATCH: I can solve all this. He is from Madrid; his father's name: Don Pedro Questo Portento* Barbinetto. Here's a letter of his to Sir Jealous, which he dropped one day; you understand Spanish, and the hand may be counterfeited. You conceive[1] me, sir?

CHARLES: My better genius, thou hast revived my drooping soul! I'll about it instantly. Come to my lodgings, and we'll concert[2] matters.

(*Exeunt.*)

SCENE IV

A garden gate, open, SCENTWELL *waiting within. Enter* SIR GEORGE AIRY.

SIR GEORGE: So this is the gate, and most invitingly open. If there should be a blunderbuss here now, what a dreadful ditty would my fall make for fools, and what a jest for the wits; how my name would be roared about streets! Well, I'll venture all.

SCENTWELL (*entering*): Hist,[3] hist, Sir George Airy!

SIR GEORGE: A female voice! Thus far I'm safe, my dear.

SCENTWELL: No, I'm not your dear, but I'll conduct you to her. Give me your hand – you must go through many a dark passage and dirty step before you arrive.

---

1 *conceive*: Understand.

2 *concert*: Arrange.

3 *Hist*: Much like 'psst', an interjection used to attract someone's attention.

SIR GEORGE: I know I must before I arrive at paradise; therefore be quick, my charming guide.

SCENTWELL: For aught you know. Come, come, your hand and away.

SIR GEORGE: Here, here child, you can't be half so swift as my desires.

(*Exeunt.*)

SCENE V

SIR FRANCIS GRIPE*'s house. Enter* MIRANDA.

MIRANDA: Well, let me reason a little with my mad self. Now, don't I transgress all rules to venture upon a man without the advice of the grave and wise? But then, a rigid knavish[1] guardian who would have married me? To whom? Even to his nauseous self, or nobody. Sir George is what I have tried in conversation, inquired into his character, am satisfied in both. Then his love – who would have given a hundred pound only to have seen a woman he had not infinitely loved? So I find my liking him has furnished me with arguments enough of his side; and now the only doubt remains whether he will come or no.

(*Enter* SCENTWELL *and* SIR GEORGE.)

SCENTWELL: That's resolved, madam, for here's the knight.

1 *knavish*: Unscrupulous.

(*Exit* SCENTWELL.)

SIR GEORGE: And do I once more behold that lovely object whose idea fills my mind and forms my pleasing dreams!

MIRANDA: What, beginning again in heroics? Sir George, don't you remember how little fruit your last prodigal oration produced? Not one bare single word in answer.

SIR GEORGE: Ha! The voice of my Incognita! Why did you take ten thousand ways to captivate a heart your eyes alone had vanquished?

MIRANDA: Prithee, no more of these flights, for our time's but short, and we must fall into business. Do you think we can agree on that same terrible bugbear, matrimony, without heartily repenting on both sides?

SIR GEORGE: It has been my wish since first my longing eyes beheld ye.

MIRANDA: And your happy ears drank in the pleasing news I had thirty thousand pound.

SIR GEORGE: Unkind! Did I not offer you in those purchased minutes to run the risk of your fortune, so you would but secure that lovely person to my arms?

MIRANDA: Well, if you have such love and tenderness (since our wooing has been short), pray reserve it for our future days, to let the world see we are lovers after wedlock – 'twill be a novelty.

SIR GEORGE: Haste, then, and let us tie the knot and prove the envied pair—

MIRANDA: Hold! Not so fast! I have provided better than to venture on dangerous experiments headlong. My guardian, trusting to my dissembled love, has given up my fortune to my own dispose, but with this proviso – that he tomorrow morning weds me. He is now gone to Doctors' Commons* for a license.

SIR GEORGE: Ha, a license!

MIRANDA: But I have planted emissaries that infallibly take him down to Epsom, under pretence that a brother usurer of his is to make him his executor – the thing on earth he covets.

SIR GEORGE: 'Tis his known character.

MIRANDA: Now, my instruments[1] confirm him – this man – is dying, and he sends me word he goes this minute; it must be tomorrow ere he can be undeceived. That time is ours.

SIR GEORGE: Let us improve it, then, and settle on our coming years endless, endless happiness.

MIRANDA: I dare not stir till I hear he's on the road – then I and my writings, the most material point, are soon removed.

SIR GEORGE: I have one favour to ask, if it lies in your power: you would be a friend to poor Charles. Though the son of this tenacious man, he is as free from all his vices as nature and a good education can make him, and, what now I have vanity enough to hope will induce you: he is the man on earth I love.

MIRANDA: I never was his enemy, and only put it on as it helped my designs on his father. If his uncle's estate ought to be in his possession, which I shrewdly suspect, I may do him a singular piece of service.

1 *instruments*: Agents, contacts.

SIR GEORGE: You are all goodness.

(*Enter* SCENTWELL.)

SCENTWELL: Oh, madam, my master and Mr Marplot are just coming into the house.

MIRANDA: Undone, undone! If he finds you here in this crisis, all my plots are unravelled.

SIR GEORGE: What shall I do? Can't I get back into the garden?

SCENTWELL: Oh, no! He comes up those stairs.

MIRANDA: Here, here, here! Can you condescend to stand behind this chimney board,[1] Sir George?

SIR GEORGE: Anywhere, anywhere, dear madam, without ceremony.

SCENTWELL: Come, come, sir, lie close.[2]

(*They put him behind the chimney board. Enter* SIR FRANCIS *and* MARPLOT, SIR FRANCIS *peeling an orange.*)

SIR FRANCIS: I could not go, though 'tis upon life and death, without taking leave of dear Chargee. Besides, this fellow buzzed in my ears that thou might'st be so desperate to shoot that wild rake which haunts the garden gate, and that would bring us into trouble, dear.

MIRANDA: So Marplot brought you back, then? I am obliged to him for that, I'm sure. (*Frowning at* MARPLOT *aside.*)

1 *chimney board*: Fireplaces were closed up in the summer, with a board placed in front of them to obscure them from view.

2 *close*: Concealed, hidden.

MARPLOT (*aside*): By her looks she means she is not obliged to me. I have done some mischief now, but what I can't imagine.

SIR FRANCIS: Well, Chargee, I have had three messengers to come to Epsom to my neighbour Squeezum's, who, for all his vast riches, is departing. (*Sighs.*)

MARPLOT: Aye, see what all you usurers must come to.

SIR FRANCIS: Peace, ye young knave! Some forty years hence I may think on't! But, Chargee, I'll be with thee tomorrow, before those pretty eyes are open. I will, I will, Chargee, I'll rouse you, i' faith. Here, Mrs Scentwell, lift up your lady's chimney board, that I may throw my peel in and not litter her chamber.

MIRANDA (*aside*): Oh my stars! What will become of us now?

SCENTWELL: Oh, pray, sir, give it me; I love it above all things in nature, indeed I do.

SIR FRANCIS: No, no, hussy, you have the green pip[1] already. I'll have no more apothecary's bills. (*Goes towards the chimney.*)

MIRANDA: Hold, hold, hold, dear Gardee! I have a… a… a… a… a monkey shut up there; and if you open it before the man comes that is to tame it, 'tis so wild 'twill break all my china,* or get away; and that would break my heart, for I am fond on't to distraction… (*in a flattering tone:*) next thee, dear Gardee.

SIR FRANCIS: Well, well, Chargee, I won't open it. She shall have her monkey, poor rogue! (*To* SCENTWELL*:*) Here, throw this peel out of the window.

---

1 *pip*: Illness (humorous).

(*Exit* SCENTWELL.)

MARPLOT: A monkey, dear madam? Let me see it – I can tame a monkey as well as the best of them all. Oh, how I love the little miniatures of man.*

MIRANDA (*striving with him*): Be quiet, mischief, and stand further from the chimney. You shall not see my monkey! Why, sure—

MARPLOT: For Heaven's sake, dear madam, let me but peep to see if it be as pretty as my Lady Fiddle-Faddle's. Has it got a chain?

MIRANDA: Not yet, but I design it one shall last its lifetime! Nay, you shall not see it. Look, Gardee, how he teases me!

SIR FRANCIS (*getting between* MARPLOT *and the chimney*): Sirrah, sirrah, let my Chargee's monkey alone, or bamboo shall fly about your ears. What, is there no dealing with you?

MARPLOT: Pugh, pox of the monkey! Here's a rout:[1] I wish he may rival you.

(*Enter a* SERVANT.)

SERVANT: Sir, they put two more horses in the coach, as you ordered, and 'tis ready at the door.

SIR FRANCIS: Well, I'm going to be executor – better for thee, jewel. Bye Chargee, one buss! I'm glad thou hast got a monkey to divert thee a little.

MIRANDA: Thank'ee, dear Gardee. Nay, I'll see you to the coach.

---

1 *rout*: Uproar, great noise.

SIR FRANCIS: That's kind, adod.

MIRANDA (*to* MARPLOT): Come along, impertinence.

(*Exeunt* MIRANDA, SIR FRANCIS *and* SERVANT.)

MARPLOT (*starting to leave, then stepping back*): Egad, I will see the monkey. Now. (*Lifts up the board, and discovers* SIR GEORGE.) Oh lord! Oh lord! Thieves, thieves, murder!

SIR GEORGE: Damn'ee, you unlucky dog! 'Tis I! Which way shall I get out? Show me instantly, or I'll cut your throat.

MARPLOT: Undone, undone! At that door there. But hold, hold, break that china, and I'll bring you off.

(SIR GEORGE *runs off at the corner and throws down some china. Re-enter* SIR FRANCIS, MIRANDA *and* SCENTWELL.)

SIR FRANCIS: Mercy on me! What's the matter?

MIRANDA: Oh, you toad! What have you done?

MARPLOT: No great harm – I beg of you to forgive me. Longing to see the monkey, I did but just raise up the board, and it flew over my shoulders, scratched all my face, broke yon china and whisked out of the window.

SIR FRANCIS: Was ever such an unlucky rogue? Sirrah, I forbid you my house. Call the servants to get the monkey again! I would stay myself to look it, but that you know my earnest business.

SCENTWELL: Oh, my lady will be the best to lure it back – all them creatures love my lady extremely.

MIRANDA: Go, go, dear Gardee – I hope I shall recover it.

SIR FRANCIS: Bye, bye, dearie. Ah, mischief, how you look now! Bye, bye. (*Exit.*)

MIRANDA: Scentwell, see him in the coach, and bring me word.

SCENTWELL: Yes, madam. (*Exit.*)

MIRANDA: So, sir, you have done your friend a signal[1] piece of service, I suppose.

MARPLOT: Why, look you, madam! If I have committed a fault, thank yourself! No man is more serviceable when I am let into a secret, nor none more unlucky at finding it out. Who could divine your meaning when you talked of a blunderbuss? Who thought of a rendezvous? And when you talked of a monkey, who the devil dreamt of Sir George?

MIRANDA: A sign you converse but little with our sex when you can't reconcile contradictions.

(*Enter* SCENTWELL.)

SCENTWELL: He's gone, madam, as fast as the coach and six can carry him.

(*Enter* SIR GEORGE.)

SIR GEORGE: Then I may appear.

MARPLOT: Dear Sir George, make my peace! On my soul, I did not think of you.

---

1 *signal*: Notable.

SIR GEORGE: I dare swear thou didst not. Madam, I beg you to forgive him.

MIRANDA: Well, Sir George, if he can be secret.

MARPLOT: Odsheart,[1] madam, I'm as secret as a priest when I'm trusted.

SIR GEORGE: Why, 'tis with a priest our business is at present.

SCENTWELL: Madam, here's Mrs Isabinda's woman to wait on you.

MIRANDA: Bring her up.

(*Enter* PATCH.)

How do'ee, Mrs Patch? What news from your lady?

PATCH: That's for your private ear, madam. Sir George, there's a friend of yours has an urgent occasion for your assistance.

SIR GEORGE: His name?

PATCH: Charles.

MARPLOT (*aside*): Ha! Then there is something afoot that I know nothing of. —I'll wait on you, Sir George.

SIR GEORGE: A third person may not be proper, perhaps. As soon as I have dispatched my own affairs I am at his service. I'll send my servant to tell him I'll wait upon him in half an hour.

MIRANDA: How come you employed in this message, Mrs Patch?

PATCH: Want of business, madam. I am discharged by my master, but hope to serve my lady still.

---

1 *Odsheart*: An exclamation (from God's heart).

MIRANDA: How, discharged? You must tell me the whole story within.

PATCH: With all my heart, madam.

MARPLOT (*aside*): Pish! Pox, I wish I were fairly out of the house. I find marriage is the end of this secret, and now I am half mad to know what Charles wants him for.

SIR GEORGE: Madam, I'm doubly pressed, by love and friendship. This exigence admits of no delay. Shall we make Marplot of the party?

MIRANDA: If you'll run the hazard, Sir George; I believe he means well.

MARPLOT (*going*): Nay, nay, for my part, I desire to be let into nothing. I'll be gone, therefore pray don't mistrust me.

SIR GEORGE (*aside*): So now has he a mind to be gone to Charles; but, not knowing what affairs he may have upon his hands at present, I'm resolved he shan't stir. —No, Mr Marplot, you must not leave us – we want a third person. (*Takes hold of him.*)

MARPLOT (*aside*): I never had more mind to be gone in my life!

MIRANDA: Come along, then; if we fail in the voyage thank yourself for taking this ill-starred gentleman on board.

SIR GEORGE:

That vessel ne'er can unsuccessful prove,
Whose freight is beauty, and whose pilot love.

(*Exeunt.*)

THE END OF THE FOURTH ACT

ACT V

SCENE I

SIR FRANCIS GRIPE*'s house. Enter* MIRANDA, PATCH *and* SCENTWELL.

MIRANDA: Well, Patch, I have done a strange, bold thing! My fate is determined, and expectation is no more. Now, to avoid the impertinence and roguery of an old man I have thrown myself into the extravagance of a young one. If he should despise, slight or use me ill, there's no remedy from a husband but the grave;* and that's a terrible sanctuary to one of my age and constitution.

PATCH: O fear not, madam, you'll find your account[1] in Sir George Airy; it is impossible a man of sense should use a woman ill, endued with beauty, wit and fortune. It must be the lady's fault if she does not wear the unfashionable name of wife easy, when nothing but complaisance and good humour is requisite on either side to make them happy.

1 *account*: An advantageous position.

MIRANDA: I long till I am out of this house, lest any accident should bring my guardian back. Scentwell, put my best jewels into the little casket, slip them into thy pocket and let us march off to Sir Jealous'.

SCENTWELL: It shall be done, madam. (*Exit.*)

PATCH: Sir George will be impatient, madam. If their plot succeeds, we shall be well received; if not, he will be able to protect us. Besides, I long to know how my young lady fares.

MIRANDA: Farewell, old Mammon, and thy detested walls; 'twill be no more 'Sweet Sir Francis' – I shall be compelled to the odious task of dissembling no longer to get my own, and coax him with the wheedling names of my 'precious', 'my dear', 'dear Gardee'.

(*Enter* SIR FRANCIS *behind.* MIRANDA *starts.*)

Oh, heavens!

SIR FRANCIS: Ah, my sweet Chargee, don't be frighted. But thy poor Gardee has been abused, cheated, fooled, betrayed, but nobody knows by whom.

MIRANDA (*aside*): Undone! Past redemption.

SIR FRANCIS: What, won't you speak to me, Chargee?

MIRANDA: I'm so surprised with joy to see you, I know not what to say.

SIR FRANCIS: Poor, dear girl! But do'ee know that my son, or some such rogue, to rob or murder me, or both, contrived this journey? For upon the road I met my neighbour Squeezum, well, and coming to town.

MIRANDA: Good lack,[1] good lack! What tricks are there in this world!

(*Enter* SCENTWELL, *with a diamond necklace in her hand, not seeing* SIR FRANCIS.)

SCENTWELL: Madam, be pleased to tie this necklace on, for I can't get it into the— (*Sees* SIR FRANCIS.)

MIRANDA (*aside*): The wench is a fool, I think! —Could you not have carried it to be mended without putting it in the box?

SIR FRANCIS: What's the matter?

MIRANDA: Only, dearie, I bid her, I bid her— Your ill usage has put everything out of my head. But won't you go, Gardee, and find out these fellows, and have them punished? And, and—

SIR FRANCIS: Where should I look them, child? No, I'll sit me down, contented with my safety, nor stir out of my own doors till I go with thee to a parson.

MIRANDA (*aside*): If he goes into his closet I am ruined. —Oh! Bless me, in this fright, I had forgot Mrs Patch.

PATCH (*aside to* MIRANDA): Aye, madam, and I stay for your speedy answer.

MIRANDA (*aside*): I must get him out of the house. Now assist me, Fortune.

SIR FRANCIS: Mrs Patch, I profess I did not see you. How dost thou do, Mrs Patch? Well, don't you repent leaving my Chargee?

---

1 *Good lack*: Expression of dismay; alack.

PATCH: Yes, everybody must love her, but I came now… (*Aside to* MIRANDA:) Madam, what did I come for? My invention is at the last ebb.

SIR FRANCIS: Nay, never whisper, tell me.

MIRANDA: She came, dear Gardee, to invite me to her lady's wedding; and you shall go with me, Gardee – 'tis to be done this moment to a Spanish merchant. Old Sir Jealous keeps on his humour – the first minute he sees her, the next he marries her.

SIR FRANCIS: Ha, ha, ha! I'd go if I thought the sight of matrimony would tempt Chargee to perform her promise: There was a smile, there was a consenting look with those pretty twinklers worth a million. Ods precious, I am happier than the great Mogul, the Emperor of China, or all the potentates that are not in wars.* Speak, confirm it, make me leap out of my skin.

MIRANDA: When one has resolved, 'tis in vain to stand 'Shall I, shall I?', 'If ever I marry…' – positively this is my wedding day.

SIR FRANCIS: Oh! Happy, happy man! Verily, I will beget a son – the first night shall disinherit that dog, Charles. I have estate enough to purchase a barony, and be the immortalising the whole family of the Gripes.

MIRANDA: Come then, Gardee, give me thy hand; let's to this house of Hymen.*

My choice is fixed, let good or ill betide.

SIR FRANCIS:

The joyful bridegroom, I—

MIRANDA:

And I the happy bride.

(*Exeunt.*)

SCENE II

SIR JEALOUS TRAFFICK*'s house. Enter* SIR JEALOUS, *meeting a* SERVANT.

SERVANT: Sir, here's a couple of gentlemen enquire for you; one of 'em calls himself Señor Diego Barbinetto.

SIR JEALOUS: Ha! Seignor Barbinetto! Admit 'em instantly! Joyful minute: I'll have my daughter married tonight.

(*Enter* CHARLES *in Spanish habit, with* SIR GEORGE, *dressed like a merchant.*)

SIR JEALOUS: *Senior, beso las manos. Vuestra merced es muy bienvenido en esta tierra.**

CHARLES: *Señor, soy el muy humilde, y muy obligado criado de vuestra merced. Mi padre envia a vuestra merced los más profondos de sus respetos, y ha commissionado este mercader Inglés de concluir un negocio que me hace el más dischoso hombre del mundo, haciendo me su yerno.**

SIR JEALOUS: I am glad on't, for I find I have lost much of my Spanish.* Sir, I am your most humble servant. Seignor Don Diego Barbinetto has informed me that you are commissioned by Seignor Don Pedro, etc., his worthy father.

SIR GEORGE: To see an affair of marriage consummated between a daughter of yours and Señor Diego Barbinetto, his son here. True, sir: such a trust is reposed in me (*gives him a letter*), as that letter will inform you. (*Aside:*) I hope 'twill pass upon him.

SIR JEALOUS: Aye, 'tis his hand. (*Seems to read.*)

SIR GEORGE (*aside*): Good. (*To* CHARLES:) You have counterfeited to a nicety, Charles.

CHARLES (*aside to* SIR GEORGE): If the whole plot succeeds as well, I'm happy.

SIR JEALOUS: Sir, I find by this that you are a man of honour and probity; I think, sir, he calls you Meanwell?

SIR GEORGE: Meanwell is my name, sir.

SIR JEALOUS: A very good name, and very significant.

CHARLES (*aside*): Yes, faith, if he knew all.

SIR JEALOUS: For to mean well is to be honest, and to be honest is the virtue of a friend, and a friend is the delight and support of human society.

SIR GEORGE: You shall find that I'll discharge the part of a friend in what I have undertaken, Sir Jealous.

CHARLES (*aside*): But little does he think to whom.

SIR GEORGE: Therefore, sir, I must entreat the presence of your fair daughter, and the assistance of your chaplain; for Señor Don Pedro strictly enjoined me to see the marriage rites performed as soon as we should arrive, to avoid the accidental overtures of Venus.*

SIR JEALOUS: Overtures of Venus!

SIR GEORGE: Aye, sir. That is, those little hawking females[1] that traverse the park and the playhouse to put off their damaged ware – they fasten upon foreigners like leeches, and watch their arrival as carefully as the Kentish men do a shipwreck. I warrant you they have heard of him already.

SIR JEALOUS: Nay, I know this town swarms with them.

1 *hawking females*: Prostitutes.

SIR GEORGE: Aye, and then you know the Spaniards are naturally amorous, but very constant – the first face fixes 'em, and it may be dangerous to let him ramble ere he is tied.

CHARLES (*aside*): Well hinted.

SIR JEALOUS: Pat to my purpose. Well, sir, there is but one thing more, and they shall be married instantly.

CHARLES (*aside*): Pray Heaven that one thing more don't spoil all.

SIR JEALOUS: Don Pedro writ me word in his last but one that he designed the sum of five thousand crowns by way of jointure[1] for my daughter, and that it should be paid into my hand upon the day of marriage—

CHARLES (*aside*): Oh, the devil!

SIR JEALOUS: In order to lodge it in some of our funds,[2] in case she should become a widow and return for England.

SIR GEORGE (*aside*): Pox on't, this is an unlucky turn. What shall I say?

SIR JEALOUS: And he does not mention one word of it in this letter.

CHARLES (*aside*): I don't know how he should.

SIR GEORGE: Humph! True, Sir Jealous; he told me such a thing, but… but… but… but he… he… he… he… he did not imagine that you would insist upon the very day, for… for… for… for money, you know, is dangerous returning by sea, and… and… and… and—

CHARLES (*aside to* SIR GEORGE): Zounds, say we have brought it in commodities.

---

1 *jointure*: The property or money given to a wife.

2 *funds*: Government funds, bonds.

SIR GEORGE: And so, sir, he has sent it in merchandise – tobacco, sugars, spices, lemons and so forth – which shall be turned into money with all expedition.[1] In the mean time, sir, if you please to accept of my bond for performance.

SIR JEALOUS: It is enough, sir. I am so pleased with the countenance of Seignor Diego and the harmony of your name that I'll take your word, and will fetch my daughter this moment. Within there!

(*Enter* SERVANT.)

Desire Mr Tackum, my neighbour's chaplain, to walk hither.

SERVANT: Yes, sir. (*Exit.*)

SIR JEALOUS: Gentlemen, I'll return in an instant. (*Exit.*)

CHARLES: Wondrous well. Let me embrace thee.

SIR GEORGE: Egad, that five thousand crowns* had like to have ruined the plot!

CHARLES: But that's over! And if Fortune throws no more rubs[2] in our way…

SIR GEORGE: Thou'lt carry the prize. But hist,[3] here he comes.

(*Enter* SIR JEALOUS, *dragging in* ISABINDA.)

SIR JEALOUS: Come along, you stubborn baggage, you, come along.

1 *expedition*: Haste.

2 *rubs*: Problems, obstacles.

3 *hist*: In this usage, 'shh!'

ISABINDA:*

Oh, hear me, sir! Hear me but speak one word –
Do not destroy my everlasting peace.
My soul abhors this Spaniard you have chose;
Nor can I wed him without being cursed.

SIR JEALOUS: How's that?

ISABINDA (*kneeling*):

Let this posture move your tender nature.
For ever will I hang upon these knees;
Nor loose my hands till you cut off my hold,
If you refuse to hear me, sir.

CHARLES (*aside*): Oh! That I could discover myself to her!

SIR GEORGE (*aside to* CHARLES): Have a care what you do. You had better trust to his obstinacy.

SIR JEALOUS: Did you ever see such a perverse slut? Off, I say! Mr Meanwell, pray help me a little.

SIR GEORGE: Rise, madam, and do not disoblige your father, who has provided a husband worthy of you – one that will love you equal with his soul, and one that you will love, when once you know him.

ISABINDA: Oh! Never, never.

Could I suspect that falsehood in my heart,
I would this moment tear it from my breast,
and straight present him with the treacherous part.

CHARLES (*aside*): Oh! My charming faithful dear!

SIR JEALOUS: Falsehood! Why, who the devil are you in love with? Ha! Don't provoke me, for by St Jago I shall beat you, housewife.

CHARLES (*aside*): Heaven forbid, for I shall infallibly discover myself if he should.

SIR GEORGE: Have patience, madam, and look at him! Why will you prepossess yourself against a man that is master of all the charms you would desire in a husband?

SIR JEALOUS: Aye, look at him, Isabinda. *Senior, pase vind adelante.**

CHARLES (*aside*): My heart bleeds to see her grieve, whom I imagined would with joy receive me. —*Señora, obligue me, vuestra merced, de su mano.**

SIR JEALOUS (*pulling up her head*): Hold up your head, hold up your head, housewife, and look at him: is there a properer, handsomer, better-shaped fellow in England, ye jade you? Ha! See, see the obstinate baggage shuts her eyes! By St Jago, I have a good mind to beat 'em out. (*Pushes her down.*)

ISABINDA:

Do, then, sir – kill me, kill me instantly.
'Tis much the kinder action of the two,
For 'twill be worse than death to wed him.

SIR GEORGE: Sir Jealous, you are too passionate. Give me leave; I'll try by gentle words to work her to your purpose.

SIR JEALOUS (*weeping*): I pray do, Mr Meanwell, I pray do; she'll break my heart. There is in that* jewels of the value of three thousand pounds, which were her mother's, and a paper wherein I have settled one half of my estate upon her now, and the whole when I die – but provided she marries this gentleman, else, by St Jago, I'll turn her out of doors to beg or starve. Tell her this, Mr Meanwell, pray do. (*Walks off.*)

SIR GEORGE (*aside*): Ha! This is beyond expectation! — Trust to me, sir: I'll lay the dangerous consequence of disobeying you at this juncture before her, I warrant you.

CHARLES (*aside*): A sudden joy runs through my heart like a propitious omen.

SIR GEORGE: Come, madam, do not blindly cast your life away just in the moment you would wish to have it.

ISABINDA: Pray cease your trouble, sir. I have no wish but sudden death to free me from this hated Spaniard. If you are his friend, inform him what I say: my heart is given to another youth, whom I love with the same strength of passion that I hate this Diego,[1] with whom, if I am forced to wed, my own hand shall cut the Gordian knot.*

SIR GEORGE: Suppose this Spaniard which you strive to shun should be the very man to whom you'd fly?

ISABINDA: Ha!

SIR GEORGE: Would you not blame your rash result, and curse those eyes that would not look on Charles?

ISABINDA: On Charles? Oh, you have inspired new life and collected every wandering sense! Where is he? Oh, let me fly into his arms! (*Rises.*)

SIR GEORGE: Hold, hold, hold! 'Sdeath, madam, you'll ruin all – your father believes him to be Señor Barbinetto. Compose yourself a little, pray, madam.

(SIR GEORGE *runs to* SIR JEALOUS.)

1 *Diego*: Spaniard.

CHARLES (*aside*): Her eyes declare she knows me.

SIR GEORGE: She begins to hear reason, sir; the fear of being turned out of doors has done it. (*Runs back to* ISABINDA.)

ISABINDA: 'Tis he! Oh, my ravished soul!

SIR GEORGE: Take heed, madam, you don't betray yourself. Seem with reluctance to consent, or you are undone. (*Runs to* SIR JEALOUS.) Speak gently to her, sir – I'm sure she'll yield; I see it in her face.

SIR JEALOUS (*returning*): Well, Isabinda, can you refuse to bless a father whose only care is to make you happy, as Mr Meanwell has informed you? Come, wipe thy eyes; nay, prithee do, or thou wilt break thy father's heart. (*Weeping:*) See, thou bringest the tears in mine to think of thy undutiful carriage to me.

ISABINDA: Oh, do not weep, sir! Your tears are like a poniard[1] to my soul. Do with me what you please; I am all obedience.

SIR JEALOUS: Ha! Then thou art my child again.

SIR GEORGE (*aside to* CHARLES): 'Tis done, and now, friend, the day's thy own.

CHARLES (*aside to* SIR GEORGE): The happiest of my life, if nothing intervene.

SIR JEALOUS: And wilt thou love him?

ISABINDA: I will endeavour it, sir.

(*Enter* SERVANT.)

SERVANT: Sir, here is Mr Tackum.

---

1 *poniard*: A small, slim dagger.

SIR JEALOUS: Show him into the parlour. *Senior, tome vind su esposa; cette momenta les junta les manos.** (*Gives her to* CHARLES.)

CHARLES (*aside*): Oh, transport! —*Señor, yo la recibo como se debe un tesoro tan grande.** (*To* ISABINDA:) Oh, my joy, my life, my soul!

(CHARLES *and* ISABINDA *embrace.*)

ISABINDA: My faithful everlasting comfort.

SIR JEALOUS: Now, Mr Meanwell, let's to the parson,
Who, by his art, will join this pair for life –
Make me the happiest father, her the happiest wife.

(*Exeunt.*)

SCENE III

Scene changes to the street before SIR JEALOUS' *door. Enter* MARPLOT, *solus.*)[1]

MARPLOT: I have hunted all over the town for Charles, but can't find him; and, by Whisper's scouting at the end of the street, I suspect he must be in this house again. I'm informed, too, that he has borrowed a Spanish habit out of the playhouse. What can it mean?

(*Enter a* SERVANT *of* SIR JEALOUS' *to him, out of the house.*)

Harkee, sir, do you belong to this house?

---

1 *solus*: Alone.

SERVANT: Yes, sir.

MARPLOT: Pray, can you tell if there be a gentleman in it in Spanish habit?

SERVANT: There is a Spanish gentleman within that is just a-going to marry my young lady, sir.

MARPLOT: Are you sure he is a Spanish gentleman?

SERVANT: I'm sure he speaks no English that I hear of.

MARPLOT: Then that can't be him I want, for 'tis an English gentleman – though I suppose he may be dressed like a Spaniard – that I enquire after.

SERVANT (*aside*): Ha! Who knows but this may be an impostor? I'll inform my master, for if he should be imposed upon, he'll beat us all round. —Pray, come in, sir, and see if this be the person you enquire for.

(*Exeunt.*)

SCENE IV

Scene changes to the inside the house. Enter MARPLOT.

MARPLOT: So, this was a good contrivance: if this be Charles, now will he wonder how I found him out.

(*Enter* SERVANT *and* SIR JEALOUS.)

SIR JEALOUS (*to the* SERVANT): What is your earnest business, blockhead, that you must speak with me before the ceremony's past? Ha! Who's this?

SERVANT: Why, this gentleman, sir, wants another gentleman in Spanish habit, he says.

SIR JEALOUS: In Spanish habit! 'Tis some friend of Seignior Don Diego's, I warrant. (*To* MARPLOT:)* Sir, I suppose you would speak with Seignior Barbinetto?

MARPLOT (*aside*): Heyday! What the devil does he say now? —Sir, I don't understand you.

SIR JEALOUS: Don't you understand Spanish, sir?

MARPLOT: Not I indeed, sir.

SIR JEALOUS: I thought you had known Seignior Barbinetto?

MARPLOT: Not I, upon my word, sir.

SIR JEALOUS: What, then you'd speak with his friend, the English merchant, Mr Meanwell?

MARPLOT: Neither, sir, not I.

SIR JEALOUS (*in an angry tone*): Why, who are you then, sir? And what do you want?

MARPLOT: Nay, nothing at all, not I, sir. (*Aside:*) Pox on him! I wish I were out. He begins to exalt[1] his voice; I shall be beaten again.

SIR JEALOUS: Nothing at all, sir! Why then, what business have you in my house? Ha?

SERVANT: You said you wanted a gentleman in Spanish habit.

MARPLOT: Why aye, but his name is neither Barbinetto nor Meanwell.

SIR JEALOUS: What is his name, then, sirrah, ha? Now I look at you again, I believe you are the rogue threatened me with half a dozen myrmidons! Speak, sir – who is it you look for? Or, or—

MARPLOT (*aside*): A terrible old dog! —Why, sir, only an honest young fellow of my acquaintance. I thought that

1 *exalt*: Raise:

here might be a ball, and that he might have been here in a masquerade. 'Tis Charles, Sir Francis Gripe's son, because I know he used to come hither sometimes.

SIR JEALOUS: Did he so? Not that I know of, I'm sure. Pray Heaven that this be Don Diego… If I should be tricked now! Ha! My heart misgives me plaguily. (*Calling off:*) Within there! Stop the marriage! (*To the* SERVANT*:*) Run, sirrah, call all my servants! I'll be satisfied that this is Seignior Pedro's son ere he has my daughter.

(*Exit* SERVANT. *Enter* SIR GEORGE *with a drawn sword between the scenes.*)*

MARPLOT: Ha, Sir George! What have I done now?

SIR GEORGE (*aside*): Ha! Marplot, here? Oh, the unlucky dog! —What's the matter, Sir Jealous?

SIR JEALOUS: Nay, I don't know the matter, Mr Meanwell.

MARPLOT (*going up to* SIR GEORGE): Upon my soul, Sir George—

SIR JEALOUS: Nay, then, I'm betrayed, ruined, undone! Thieves, traitors, rogues! (*Offers*[1] *to go in.*) Stop the marriage, I say!

SIR GEORGE: I say, go on, Mr Tackum! Nay, no ent'ring here – I guard this passage, old gentleman. The act and deed were both your own, and I'll see 'em signed, or die for't.

(*Enter* SERVANTS.)

---

1 *offers*: Makes to.

SIR JEALOUS: A pox on the act and deed! (*To the* SERVANTS:) Fall on, knock him down!

SIR GEORGE: Aye, come on, scoundrels! I'll prick your jackets for you.

SIR JEALOUS (*beating* MARPLOT): Zounds, sirrah, I'll be revenged on you!

SIR GEORGE: Aye, there your vengeance is due. Ha, ha!

MARPLOT: Why, what do you beat me for? I han't married your daughter!

SIR JEALOUS: Rascals! Why don't you knock him down?

SERVANT: We are afraid of his sword, sir – if you'll take that from him, we'll knock him down presently.

(*Enter* CHARLES *and* ISABINDA.)

SIR JEALOUS: Seize her, then.

CHARLES: Rascals, retire – she's my wife. Touch her if you dare; I'll make dog's meat of you.

SIR JEALOUS: Ah! Downright English! Oh, oh, oh, oh!

(*Enter* SIR FRANCIS GRIPE, MIRANDA, PATCH, SCENTWELL *and* WHISPER.)

SIR FRANCIS: Into the house of joy we enter without knocking. Ha! I think 'tis the house of sorrow, Sir Jealous.

SIR JEALOUS: Oh, Sir Francis! Are you come? What, was this your contrivance, to abuse, trick and chouse me of my child?

SIR FRANCIS: My contrivance! What do you mean?

SIR JEALOUS: No, you don't know your son there in Spanish habit.

SIR FRANCIS: How! My son in Spanish habit? Sirrah, you'll come to be hanged! Get out of my sight, ye dog! Get out of my sight.

SIR JEALOUS: Get out of your sight, sir? Get out with your bags![1] Let's see what you'll give him now to maintain my daughter on.

SIR FRANCIS: Give him? He shall be never the better for a penny of mine – and you might have looked after your daughter better, Sir Jealous. Tricked, quotha? Egad, I think you designed to trick me: but look ye, gentlemen, I believe I shall trick you both. This lady is my wife, do you see? And my estate shall descend only to the heirs of her body.

SIR GEORGE: Lawfully begotten by me – I shall be extremely obliged to you, Sir Francis.

SIR FRANCIS: Ha, ha, ha, ha! Poor Sir George! You see, your project was of no use. Does not your hundred pound stick in your stomach? Ha, ha, ha!

SIR GEORGE: No, faith, Sir Francis, this lady has given me a cordial for that. (*Takes* MIRANDA *by the hand.*)

SIR FRANCIS: Hold, sir, you have nothing to say to this lady!

SIR GEORGE: Nor you nothing to do with my wife, sir.

SIR FRANCIS: Wife, sir!

MIRANDA: Aye, really, Guardian, 'tis even so. I hope you'll forgive my first offence.

SIR FRANCIS: What, have you choused me out of my consent, and your writings then, mistress? Ha!

MIRANDA: Out of nothing but my own, Guardian.

---

1 *bags*: Money bags.

SIR JEALOUS: Ha, ha, ha! 'Tis some comfort at least to see you are over-reached as well as myself. Will you settle your estate upon your son now?

SIR FRANCIS: He shall starve first.

MIRANDA: That I have taken care to prevent. There, sir, is the writings of your uncle's estate, which has been your due these three years. (*Gives* CHARLES *papers.*)

CHARLES: I shall study to deserve this favour.

SIR FRANCIS: What, have you robbed me too, mistress? Egad, I'll make you restore 'em! Huswife, I will so.

SIR JEALOUS: Take care I don't make you pay the arrears, sir. 'Tis well it's no worse, since 'tis no better. Come, young man, seeing thou hast outwitted me, take her, and bless you both.

CHARLES: I hope, sir, you'll bestow your blessing too; 'tis all I'll ask. (*Kneels.*)

SIR FRANCIS: Confound you all! (*Exit.*)

MARPLOT: Mercy upon us! How he looks!

SIR GEORGE: Ha, ha! Ne'er mind his curses, Charles; thou'lt thrive not one jot the worse for 'em. Since this gentleman is reconciled, we are all made happy.

SIR JEALOUS: I always loved precaution, and took care to avoid dangers. But when a thing was past, I ever had philosophy to be easy.

CHARLES: Which is the true sign of a great soul. I loved your daughter, and she me, and you shall have no reason to repent her choice.

ISABINDA: You will not blame me, sir, for loving my own country best.

MARPLOT: So here's everybody happy, I find, but poor Pilgarlic.[1] I wonder what satisfaction I shall have for being cuffed, kicked and beaten in your service.

SIR JEALOUS: I have been a little too familiar with you, as things are fallen out; but since there's no help for't, you must forgive me.

MARPLOT: Egad, I think so – but provided that you be not so familiar for the future.

SIR GEORGE: Thou hast been an unlucky rogue.

MARPLOT: But very honest.

CHARLES: That I'll vouch for, and freely forgive thee.

SIR GEORGE: And I'll do you one piece of service more, Marplot – I'll take care that Sir Francis make you master of your estate.

MARPLOT: That will make me as happy as any of you.

PATCH: Your humble servant begs leave to remind you, madam.

ISABINDA: Sir, I hope you'll give me leave to take Patch into favour again.

SIR JEALOUS: Nay, let your husband look to that – I have done with my care.

CHARLES: Her own liberty shall always oblige me. Here's nobody but honest Whisper and Mrs Scentwell to be provided for now. It shall be left to their choice to marry, or keep their services.

WHISPER: Nay, then, I'll stick to my master.

SCENTWELL: Coxcomb! And I prefer my lady before a footman.

---

1 *poor Pilgarlic*: 'Poor old me'.

SIR JEALOUS: Hark, I hear music! The fiddlers smell a wedding. What say you, young fellows? Will ye have a dance?

SIR GEORGE: With all my heart; call 'em in!

(*Enter* MUSICIANS. *A dance.*)

SIR JEALOUS: Now let us in and refresh our selves with a cheerful glass, in which we'll bury all animosities; and:

By my example, let all parents move,
And never strive to cross their children's love,
But still submit that care to providence above.

(*Exeunt.*)

FINIS

EPILOGUE

In me you see one busybody more,
Though you may have enough of one before.
With epilogues, the busybody's way,
We strive to help; but sometimes mar a play.
At this mad sessions,[1] half condemned ere tried,*
Some,* in three days, have been turned off, and died.
In spite of parties,[2] their attempts are vain,
For, like false prophets, they ne'er rise again.
Too late, when cast, your favour one beseeches,
And epilogues prove execution speeches.
Yet sure I spy no busybodies here;
And one may pass, since they do ev'rywhere.
Sour critics, time and breath, and censures, waste,
And balk your pleasure to refine your taste.
One busy don ill-timed high tenets preaches,
Another yearly shows himself in speeches.
Some snivelling cits[3] would have a peace for spite,
To starve those warriors who so bravely fight,*

---

1 *sessions*: That is, judicial sessions.

2 *parties*: That is, audience plants who tried to encourage applause.

3 *cits*: Citizens.

Still of a foe upon his knees, afraid,
Whose well-banged troops want money, heart and bread.
Old beaux, who none, not ev'n themselves, can please,
Are busy still, for nothing but to tease.
The young, so busy to engage a heart,
The mischief done, are busy most to part.
Ungrateful wretches, who still cross one's will,
When they more kindly might be busy still!
One to a husband, who ne'er dreamt of horns,
Shows how dear spouse with friend his brows adorns.*
Th'officious tell-tale fool (he should repent it)
Parts three kind souls that lived at peace contented.
Some with law quirks set houses by the ears;
With physic one what he would heal impairs.
Like that dark mobbed-up[1] fry, that neighb'ring curse,
Who to remove love's pain, bestow a worse.
Since then this meddling tribe infest the age,
Bear one a while, exposed upon the stage.
Let none but busybodies vent their spite!
And, with good humour, pleasure crown the night!

1 *mobbed-up*: Robed, concealed.

NOTE ON THE TEXT

The text of this edition is based on that of the first published edition of 1709, which is widely considered to be the authoritative text; the play was reprinted many times, and many great changes were made in subsequent editions, which are not necessarily considered authorised. Capitalisation and italicisation, spelling, punctuation and grammar have been corrected and made consistent throughout, and contractions that make no difference to pronunciation (such as banish'd) have been spelt out in full to make the text more approachable for the modern reader. As was conventional at the time, many of the stage notes were given after the action they direct; in this edition they have been moved up to their conventional position in front of the directed action. Where stage notes indicate an aside, an em dash (—) has been used to demonstrate where the speaker ends the aside. Various sections are set as poetry in the original text; this has been preserved to retain the poetic style Centlivre intended. The Spanish in the play is often misspelt in the original; where errors are problematic we have made corrections, except for in the speech of Sir Jealous (see second note to p. 50).

NOTES

6 *Venice Preserved*: A reference to the 1682 tragedy by Thomas Otway (1652–85).

7 *The last character… Newcastle*: Centlivre may have drawn inspiration from *Sir Martin Mar-All, or, The Feign'd Innocence* (1667) by John Dryden (1631–1700); the 'Duchess of Newcastle' refers to Margaret Lucas Cavendish (1623–73), a philosopher, writer and playwright, although the character in question is unknown.

9 *the right… Privy Council*: John Somers (1651–1716) was an English Whig politician, who was Lord President of the Council (1708–10) when this play was published, formerly Lord Keeper of the Great Seal of England (1693–97) and Lord Chancellor (1697–1700). 'Her Majesty' is Queen Anne (1665–1714, r. 1702–07).

9 *heathenish poets*: That is, ancient Greek and Roman poets.

9 *Apollo*: A Greek god associated with poetic inspiration.

9 *that council*: That is, the Privy Council (see first note to this page).

10 *Lelius and Scipio*: Gaius Laelius Sapiens (b. *c.*188 BC) was a Roman statesman and close friend of Roman general Scipio Aemilianus (185–*c.*129 BC), patron of writers and philosophers.

10 *Terence's*: Publius Terentius Afer (*c.*190–*c.*159 BC) was a Roman playwright. Born a slave, Terence was brought to Rome by his owner, a senator, who educated him and, impressed by his talent, freed him.

11 *By the author of Tunbridge Walks*: That is, the English writer Thomas Baker (*c.*1680–1749), writer of the pioneering 1703 comedy *Tunbridge Walks*. Interestingly, the play was notable for a homosexual character, Maiden, described as 'a nice fellow that values himself upon his effeminacies'. Many critics have drawn similarities between Maiden and Marplot; perhaps Centlivre asked Baker write the prologue to draw attention to this.

11 *modern prophets were exposed of late*: A reference to the 1709 play *The Modern Prophets, or, New Wit for a Husband, a Comedy* by Thomas D'Urfey (1653–1723), which was not a great success. In the preface, D'Urfey takes aim at Thomas Baker's works, saying that one of his plays was 'deservedly hissed' at during its opening night.

11 *the wished-for peace... will cease*: A reference to the War of the Spanish Succession (1701–14), triggered by the death of Charles II of Spain, in which Britain was embroiled.

11 *The grand monarch may wish... lose his own*: This is likely referring to Louis XIV of France (1638–1715, r. 1643–1715), and his (grand)son Philip of Anjou (Philip V of Spain, 1683–1746, r. 1700–24), who was the king of Spain during the War of the Spanish Succession (see previous note). In 1708–09 France had been hit by severe financial troubles, so this line is most likely meant to suggest that Louis should like to come to Spain's aid, but is not in a position to be able to do so.

11 *But players in summer have a dismal case*: It was common at the time for fashionable society to leave London for the summer, in favour of the countryside or spa towns, and so the audiences in London theatres were greatly reduced.

11 *Since your appearance only is our act of grace*: Baker means audiences were the actors' only source of income.

12 *city wives*: That is, wives of those working in the City of London, largely merchants, as opposed to gentlewomen.

12 *Tunbridge*: Tunbridge Wells in Kent, a fashionable spa town where visitors would 'take the waters'.

12 *Gay city wives at Tunbridge… conceive*: Probably referring to the bawdy poem 'Tunbridge Wells' by John Wilmot, Earl of Rochester (1647–80), libertine, poet and courtier of King Charles II (1630–85, r. 1660–85): 'From these the waters got the reputation of good assistants unto generation.' The suggestion is that Tunbridge Wells' reputation for restoring fertility is due to the intermingling of city wives and courtiers staying there, rather than any power in the waters.

12 *Cupid's Gardens*: A reference to Cuper's Gardens, pleasure gardens on the south side of the Thames in London, looking across the river to Somerset House.

12 *Fair Dorinda*: A reference to a song in *Camilla* ('Fair Dorinda, happy, happy; happy may'st thou ever be; the stars that smile on happy days, may they all now smile on thee'), an opera by the Italian composer Giovanni Bononcini (1670–1747), which was first performed in London at Drury Lane on the 30th of April 1706, in an English translation by Owen Swiny (1676–1754). It was very popular, also appearing in *The Beaux' Stratagem* by George Farquhar (1677–1707) in 1707.

12 *'Tis tattling all, like Isaac Bickerstaff*: A reference to a pseudonym of the writer and Anglican cleric Jonathan Swift (1667–45), which he invented in order to play a hoax on John Partridge (1644–*c.*1714), a famous astrologer who gave annual predictions of deaths of notable individuals. In January 1708, angered by a comment Partridge had made about the Church, 'Bickerstaff' predicted Partridge's death on the 29th of March; when that date arrived he published a confirmation of Partridge's death. Partridge published a letter announcing that he was, in fact, not dead, but Swift claimed it to be untrue, and the hoax persisted. The character Bickerstaff was picked up by Sir Richard Steele (*c.*1672–1729) in his short-lived journal *The Tatler*.

12 *Since war and places claim the bards that write*: That is, the male writers are at war or out of town courting political favour and positions of power.

13 *Quem tulit ad… ep. 1*: A quote from Horace's *Epistularum liber secundus* (*Second Book of Epistles*, published 14 BC), traditionally translated as 'Him, whom glory in her airy car has brought upon the stage, the careless spectator dispirits, the attentive renders more diligent: so slight, so small a matter it is, which overturns or raises a mind covetous of praise!' (trans. Christopher Smart (1722–71), published 1756.)

14 *Drawer*: That is, a barman.

15 *The park*: St James's Park.

15 *A-birding*: Literally, 'catching birds' – but the suggestion is that Sir George is hunting women rather than fowl. This is perhaps also a nod to the Royal Aviary, which was in St James's Park, expanded by King Charles II.

15 *a person… unfashionable hours*: It was fashionable to been seen perambulating in St James's Park, but usually only after dinner. Charles is suggesting that it is a forbidden love that has Sir George 'hunting' at a time when he would not expect to be seen by society figures.

15 *a calculation of my nativity*: That is, a horoscope.

16 *below*: On earth.

16 *the Jew my father*: Reflective of anti-Semitic views of the time that portrayed Jews as money-grabbing.

17 *thirty thousand pound*: That is, her financial worth, which would become her husband's property upon marriage.

17 *Prester John's dominions*: A legendary Christian king who ruled a land somewhere in the East – thought to be either India or Central Asia, or perhaps Ethiopia.

17 *a brown musket*: That is, he will join the army.

18 *for that contempt*: i.e. because he does not consider her beautiful.

19 *A good assurance*: A rebuke for addressing Charles so familiarly.

19 *Whigs, or Jacks, or High-Flyers, or Low-Flyers, or Levellers*: Various political groups: Whigs were the political party in opposition to the Tories; Jacks, short for Jacobites, supported the return of the House of Stuart to the throne; High-Flyers supported and upheld High Church values (and was often shorthand for Tory), as opposed to Low-Flyers, who supported Low Church principles (and were probably Whig); and Levellers (flourishing much earlier – from around 1640 to 1650) supported a form of populism, whereby the governance of the country would be entirely decided by the House of Commons.

20 *I presume this... by his scars*: That is, from the battlefield (see third and fourth notes to p. 11).

20 *Groom Porters*: An office at Court that provided dice and cards and oversaw any disputes that arose.

20 *North Briton*: i.e. a Scotsman.

20 *Now the Deel... yer wem!*: In Scots, roughly, 'The Devil take my soul, sir, if you touch your sword I'll run you through!'

20 *a bow from the side box*: A public display of friendship, in the form of a bow from his box at the theatre.

21 *deliver a message with an air of business*: That is, deliver a romantic letter but pretend it's merely business correspondence.

22 *make the compliment*: Make the generous gesture to the merchant, a social inferior.

23 *I'll make one*: i.e. I'll be one of their number.

23 *Isabinda's Spanish father*: Not literally – see the description of Sir Jealous in the character list (see p. 14).

26 *old Argus*: Guardian. From the Greek mythological watchman with a hundred eyes, Argos.

27 *I wish it ben't for the first night's lodging*: That is, Patch hopes it's not for the opportunity of being the first man to lie with Miranda, a virgin.

27 *The favour!*: Miranda clearly reads this as confirmation that her guardian is prostituting her.

28 *ten minutes*: Later, when the meeting takes place (see pp. 41–47), the agreed time is apparently one hour, which seems consistent, so perhaps this is a mistake.

29 *Incognita*: That is, a woman whose identity has been concealed; this suggests Miranda has put on a mask.

30 *Remember you are in the park, child*: The park could be a debauched or dangerous place to be when deserted.

33 *Gardee*: That is, guardian. Likewise, Fir Francis uses 'Chargee', as in 'charge', since she is his ward.

33 *thou shalt outshine the Queen's box on an opera night*: That is, he will give her more finery and glittering jewellery than seen on those in the royal box at the opera house.

34 *the envy of the ring (for I will carry thee to Hyde Park)*: The ring was a circular horse-riding track in Hyde Park, where it was fashionable to be seen.

36 *To fine for sheriff*: At the time persons of good social standing could be chosen as sheriff. However, it was not fashionable to have an occupation; and by paying a fee one could escape these duties.

39 *this is no offer of a father*: That is, it is not a worthy proposition.

40 *Mammon*: A Biblical character associated with wealth. This is possibly a reference to the greedy fallen angel in *Paradise Lost* (1667) by John Milton (1608–74).

41 *Well, young Timon*: A reference to the titular character of Shakespeare's 1606 play *Timon of Athens*, who fritters away his money.

45 *Turns on her side*: That is, he turns about so he is facing the same direction as Miranda while he impersonates her.

47 *Actaeon's horns she means shall crown thy head*: A reference to Greek mythology, where a young hunter, Actaeon, stumbles upon the goddess Artemis while she is bathing in the woods. In a rage, she transforms him into a stag, and he is hunted down and killed by his own hounds. The sign of the horns was used to suggest cuckoldry.

48 *Why don't you… to be let?*: That is, 'Could you advertise more overtly to passers-by?'

48 *ratifia, persico, cinnamon, citron and spirit of claret*: Popular alcoholic drinks.

49 *Asgill's translation*: A reference to the writer and politician John Asgill (1659–1738), whose 1700 pamphlet *An Argument Proving that According to the Covenant of Eternal Life Revealed in the Scriptures Man May Be Translated From Hence Into that Eternal Life, Without Passing Through Death: Altho' the Humane Nature of Christ Himself Could Not Be Thus Translated Till He Had Passed Through Death* caused uproar, causing his expulsion from the Irish House of Commons.

49 *If we had but... have in Spain*: That is, young Roman Catholics would have been visited by priests to hear their confession, allowing for the possibility of illicit go-betweens – a stock character in drama of the age.

50 *a red coat and a feather*: That is, an officer.

50 *Signeur Barbinetto*: Sir Jealous' Spanish is not particularly good, as he later notes (see p. 103: 'I find I have lost much of my Spanish'), so his misspelling of 'señor' here evokes a mangled pronunciation, which he seems unable to remember how to pronounce. The name of the character Barbinetto is also spelt slightly differently across the first edition, with and without the 'r'; since Centlivre's names all have meaning, we have opted to use the 'Barbinetto' form, which appears to contain several meanings – 'barba', beard (both 'bearded' and 'disguised'), 'barbeta', fool (an actor).

50 *Grand Signior's mistress*: A title given to the Sultan of the Ottoman Empire; at this time, Ahmed III (1673–1736), who ruled from 1703 until 1730.

52 *pressed into the service*: That is, forced to join the army.

54 *Thatched House*: A popular tavern in St James's Street, Westminster, noted as a club meeting venue and favoured watering hole of notable figures.

57 *I have taken a thousand pound upon my uncle's estate*: That is, borrowed against.

59 *I'll equip him for the opera*: He is threatening to castrate him.

65 *I suppose make a bonfire of your own act and deed*: That is, upon her marrying, as her guardian Sir Francis would relinquish responsibility over her estate, only to regain it as her husband.

67 *cruel, hard-hearted Jew*: See second note to p. 16.

68 *eighteen*: That is, an eighteen-year-old.

69 *the son of a whetstone*: This is thought to allude to an archaic practice of hanging a whetstone around the neck of a liar – Marplot is saying he is sure he speaks the truth.

69 *consider the market lasts all the year*: That is, when they're married Miranda will be available to Sir Frances the year round.

69 *O! Mihi praeteritos referet si Jupiter Annos*: A quote from Virgil's *Aeneid*, which loosely translates as, 'Oh, if only Jupiter would restore my bygone years!' (In Roman mythology Jupiter was king of the gods.)

73 *thus en cavalier*: So calmly; bravely, like a soldier.

76 *Puts it besides*: That is, she puts it beside her pocket by mistake, rather than in it.

77 *He wants the eyes of Argus*: See note to p. 26.

82 *Humph, humph*: Throat-clearing noises.

82 *would the key was turned of you once*: That is, 'If only we could lock you out.'

82 *Why, you are atop of the house, and you are down in the cellar*: That is, Isabinda is playing very high and Patch is singing very low.

83 *Who waits there?*: Patch is calling for the servants who would be waiting by the door.

84 *Here lies the charm*: That is, Isabinda.

84 *Here, here, madam, smell to this*: Patch is presumably offering Isabinda smelling salts to bring her out of her swoon.

86 *I am immured to the frowns of fortune*: This slightly strange construct is in Centlivre's text; many editions presume it is an error, and should read 'I am inured to' ('I am accustomed to'). We have left the original here, as perhaps Charles is suggesting a dual meaning – he is accustomed to being trapped by the frowns of fortune.

87 *how attended*: i.e. how many servants he has.

87 *Questo Portento*: This appears to be nonsense, but is perhaps meant to mean something like 'of great significance'.

90 *Doctors' Commons*: A reference to the College of Doctors of Law in London (thought to be formed *c.*1511 and dissolved in 1858), which oversaw marriage licences and other such law.

92 *monkey shut up there… break all my china*: A reference to the then-infamous 'china scene' in *The Country Wife* (1675) by William Wycherley (1641–1716), where the libertine Horner, who has been posing as a eunuch, uses the word 'china' to discuss his sexual prowess. The suggestion here is that there is a wild animal (which would evoke ideas of sexuality in the contemporary audience member's mind) hidden, which, before being tamed by the vicar, could get out and have his way with her.

93 *miniatures of man*: Possibly a reference to a poem by the Earl of Rochester (see third note to p. 12), 'A Letter from Artemisa in the Town to Chloe in the Country', in which Artemisa describes a lady who says to her monkey, 'Kiss me, thou curious miniature of man; How odd thou art, how pretty, how japan: Oh! I could live and die with thee.'

99 *there's no remedy from a husband but the grave*: Until 1857 only men could file for divorce, and even then it could only be granted by an Act of Parliament, at great expense.

102 *great Mogul… all the potentates that are not in wars*: The 'Great Mogul' was the Emperor of the Mughal Empire, who ruled from Delhi. Sir Francis suggests that he is as happy as any great ruler whose fortune is safe.

102 *house of Hymen*: That is, church; Hymen was the Greek god of marriage.

103 *Senior, beso las manos… muy bienvenido en esta tierra*: Roughly, 'Sir, I kiss your hands. your grace is very welcome in these lands.'

103 *Señor, soy… su yerno*: 'Sir, I am your grace's very humble, and very obliged servant. My father sends your grace his deepest respects, and has hired this English merchant to conclude a business that makes me the happiest man in the world: making me your son-in-law.'

103 *I am glad on't, for I find I have lost much of my Spanish*: As previously revealed (see second note to p. 50), Sir Jealous' Spanish is not very good, so he is glad to have the English merchant on hand to translate.

104 *overtures of Venus*: Venus was the Greek goddess of love and beauty; Sir George suggests that the marriage should take place before Don Diego's head is turned.

106 *five thousand crowns*: In the original, this read 'five thousand pounds', which is been considered an error.

107 *Isabinda*: Here Isabinda switches to blank verse, echoing the style of a tragedy, which she obviously feels her situation to be.

108 *Senior, pase vind adelante*: 'Sir, step forward.'

108 *Señora, obligue me, vuestra merced, de su mano*: 'My lady, oblige me, your grace, your hand.'

108 *There is in that*: Sir Jealous is clearly gesturing to a box or chest of jewellery.

109 *shall cut the Gordian knot*: That is, she will kill herself if she is forced to marry Barbinetto.

111 *Senior, tome vind su esposa; cette momenta les junta les manos*: Roughly (and confusedly), 'Sir, take your wife; this moment joins your hands.'

111 *Señor, yo la recibo como se debe un tesoro tan grande*: Roughly, 'Sir, I receive such a great treasure in the manner one ought to' – that is, properly.

113 *To Marplot*: Judging by Marplot's apparent confusion and reply, it appears that Sir Jealous delivers this in Spanish.

114 *between the scenes*: That is, between the two groups of people.

121 *half condemned ere tried*: *The Busybody* suffered from bad reviews before it was staged, with critics deriding it based on its being written by a woman.

121 *Some*: That is, some plays.

121 *Some snivelling cits… who so bravely fight*: Centlivre does not seem to think much of those who are calling for an end to the War of the Spanish Succession.

122 *horns… his brows adorns*: That is, he is cuckolded. (See note to p. 47.)

BIOGRAPHICAL NOTE

ON SUSANNA CENTLIVRE

Like so many women of her era, relatively little is known for certain about Susanna Centlivre. The majority of the information on record is drawn from the account published in the *Poetical Register* of 1719 by the writer and biographer Giles Jacob (1686–1744), which he claimed came directly from Centlivre, although this was never corroborated.

It is thought that Centlivre was born in around 1670 in Whaplode, Lincolnshire, born the daughter of a dissenter and Parliamentarian, William Freeman of Holbeach, and his wife, Anne, the daughter of a gentleman from Lynn Regis, Norfolk. After a mean start to life – it is thought her mother died when she was only about three, her father some time later, and she suffered at the hands of cruel step-parents – Centlivre left home at about fifteen years old.

What happened in between this juncture and her arrival on the London stage is a matter of myth. The most likely version of events is thought to be that she met a group of roving actors in Stamford, which she joined, finding fame for her 'breeches roles'. Further information was recorded by John Mottley (1692–1750) in his *A Compleat List of All the English Dramatic Poets* (1747), although some of it seems quite romanticised. He described the Tory politician and poet Anthony Hammond (1668–1738) finding Centlivre weeping by the roadside, and so conveyed her to his college, St John's, Cambridge, where he disguised her as his 'Cousin Jack', allowing her to study alongside him. Whatever the veracity of this story, it is clear that Centlivre took her education upon herself, and had an interest in writing from an early age.

She soon came to the attention of a Mr Fox, a nephew of Sir Stephen Fox (1627–1716), a politician and former courtier of Charles II, who she was romantically engaged with, and possibly married to, at the age of about sixteen. Sadly, he died a mere year later, after which Centlivre met – and is thought to have married – an army officer by the name of Carroll; this marriage lasted little longer than the previous one, as he was killed only about eighteen months later, it is thought, in a duel.

Details are sparse from this point, but it seems that Centlivre spent the vast majority of her time reading, as well as acting, for money, as her work demonstrates a great awareness of literary works, particularly poetry, and she is thought to have been able to read French, a skill she perhaps honed at this time.

It was in 1700 that Centlivre's writing first came to anyone's attention, when she contributed a verse to *The Nine Muses*, a tribute book published after the great playwright John Dryden died, and she had letters printed (under the name 'Astraea', the pen name of Aphra Behn, possibly as an act of homage, possibly to attract attention) in *Familiar and Courtly Letters* (1700) and *Letters of Wit, Politicks and Morality* (1701). At the same time, her first play – *The Perjur'd Husband: or, The Adventures of Venice* – was given an airing at Drury Lane, and met with encouraging success. Largely due to the success of this play, Centlivre managed to grow her friendship circle to include many notable literary names, which appears to have been a source of encouragement for her writing.

Over the next few years she wrote a string of relatively successful plays (most of which were slotted into low-risk parts of the theatre calendar – see penultimate note to p. 11): *The Beau's Duel* and *The Stolen Heiress* in 1702, *Love's Contrivance* in 1703 and *The Gamester* and *The Basset Table* in 1705. Apart from *The Perjur'd Husband*, the plays did not advertise the sex of the author, and it was not until *The Basset Table* that reference was made to the fact that Centlivre, a woman, wrote the play – and even that was just in the epilogue.

Nonetheless, her success continued with her next play, *Love at a Venture*, which was well received, and was considered good enough by her contemporary Colley Cibber (1671–1757) to plagiarise in his 1707 play *The Double Gallant*; due to its popularity Centlivre took the play on tour.

Her writing had turned more political by this point, with *The Gamester* and *The Basset Table* aimed at reforming gamblers; and later that year she had *The Platonick Lady* performed, which took aim at society's rejection of female writers. She wrote:

> A play secretly introduced to the house, whilst the author remains unknown, is approved by everybody: the actors cry it up, and are in expectation of a great run; the bookseller of a second edition, and the scribbler of a sixth night; but if by chance the plot's discovered, and the brat found fatherless, immediately it flags in the opinion of those that extolled it before, and the bookseller falls in his price, with this reason only: it is a woman's.

The following year apparently saw Centlivre on the road again, this time acting, playing a breeches role in a revival of the 1677 play *The Rival Queens* by Nathaniel Lee (*c.*1653–92), and it is thought that she met her husband Joseph Centlivre (d. *c.*1725), a cook in the royal kitchens, at a performance for Queen Anne at Windsor Castle. They married soon after, in April 1707. It is not clear where they lived for the first few years of marriage, but they were able to move to a well-to-do residence on the corner of Buckingham Court, Spring Gardens (just off Trafalgar Square) in 1712.

Although financially much more secure, Centlivre continued to write, returning to the theatre with her most successful comedy, *The Busybody*, in 1709. The play ran for almost a fortnight, a runaway success for the time. Next came *The Man's Bewitched*, another politically leaning play, this time satirising Tory gentlemen in the countryside, which incensed the editors at the *Female Tatler*, a weekly paper, which ran 'an interview' with Centlivre, in which the playwright lambasts the acting company. It took Centlivre some work to convince the cast that it was a hoax. Undaunted by the reaction to her political works, the same year she wrote *A Bickerstaff's Burying*, a further Whiggish play.

Returning to familiar ground, betting on her success with *The Busybody*, she penned a sequel, *Marplot in Lisbon, or, The Second Part of the Busybody*, adapting the world she had previously created to carry anti-Tory sentiment. Sadly, it was not the same success.

Again, undaunted, Centlivre penned many more works with a political bent over the following years, starting with *The Perplex'd Lovers* in 1712 – which was, again, not a huge success, and the theatre banned the epilogue because they were concerned about the backlash.

Next, in April 1714, came *The Wonder*, dedicated to the Duke of Cambridge (better known today as King George II). At this point Queen Anne was still on the throne, so this was a daring show of loyalty to the House of Hanover; luckily, George I ascended to the throne just a few months later, in August. Despite, this time, the political bent, *The Wonder* was a great success. Encouraged, Centlivre continued in the same vein, publishing *The Humour of Elections*, *A Gotham Election* (which was never performed, as the Master of Revels refused to grant it a licence due to its political sentiment) and *A Wife Well Manag'd* in 1715.

Centlivre had by now reached great fame, and the literary and political attacks heightened – not least from Alexander Pope, who disparagingly referred to her as 'The Cook's Wife of Buckingham Court' and the 'slipshod Muse'. Perhaps due to these attacks, she partnered with Nicholas Rowe (1674–1718), then Poet Laureate, to write *The Cruel Gift*, her first heroic drama, which was well received. Next she returned to working alone, bringing out *A Bold Stroke for a Wife* in 1718 to great acclaim.

The following year, Centlivre fell ill (it is not known what she suffered from), and, although she continued to write, her output was greatly reduced, with only a handful of poems appearing in print over the next few years but for her last play, *The Artifice*, which appeared in 1722. Soon after, on the 1st of December 1723, she died at home in Buckingham Court, and was buried at the actors' church at St Paul's, Covent Garden.

Although her reputation suffered at the hands of some critics – both for acting in male roles and for daring to write as a woman – she continued, unabashed, and her legacy of some nineteen plays, performed well into the nineteenth century as often as Shakespeare's, speaks for itself.

MORE CLASSIC THEATRE FROM
RENARD PRESS

ISBN: 9781913724061
Paperback
£7.99 • 160pp

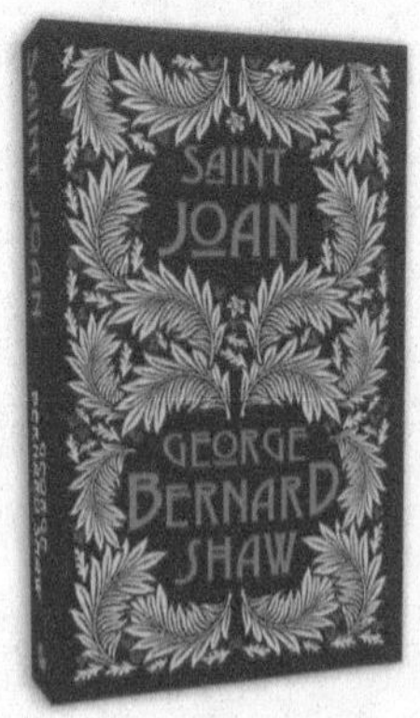

ISBN: 9781913724658
Paperback
£7.99 • 256pp

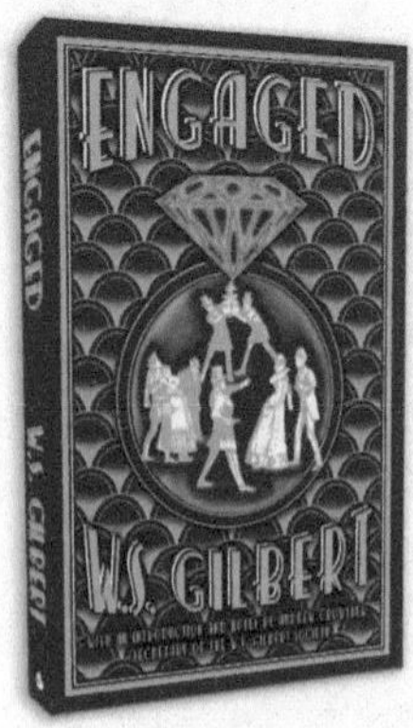

ISBN: 9781913724429
Paperback
£7.99 • 128pp

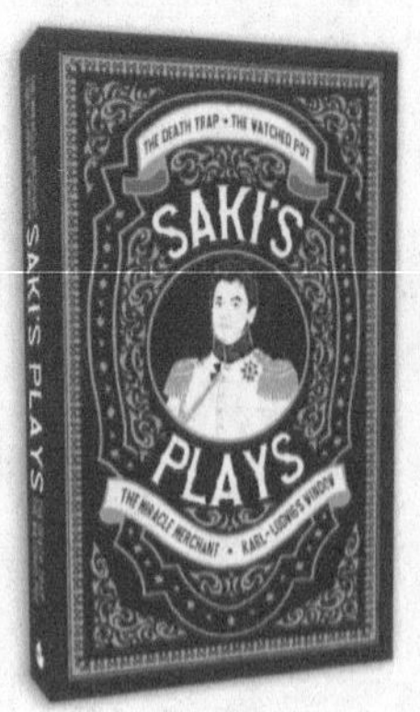

ISBN: 9781913724696
Paperback
£6.99 • 128pp

ISBN: 9781913724054
Paperback with gold foil
£7.99 • 128pp

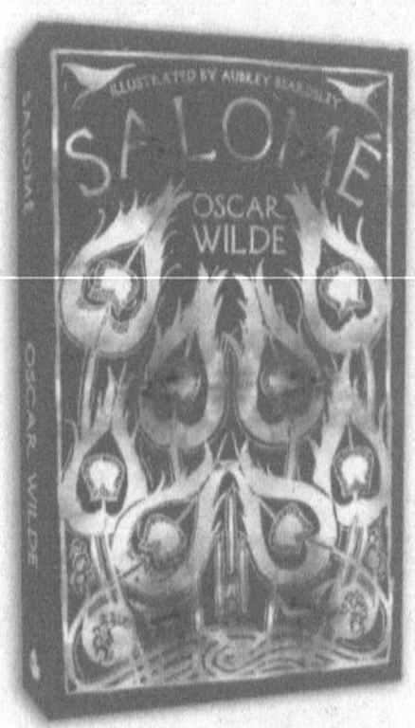

ISBN: 9781913724368
Paperback with gold foil
£7.99 • 96pp

DISCOVER THE FULL COLLECTION AT
WWW.RENARDPRESS.COM

www.ingramcontent.com/pod-product-compliance
Lightning Source LLC
Chambersburg PA
CBHW010558170726
48285CB00011B/2959

* 9 7 8 1 9 1 3 7 2 4 6 7 2 *